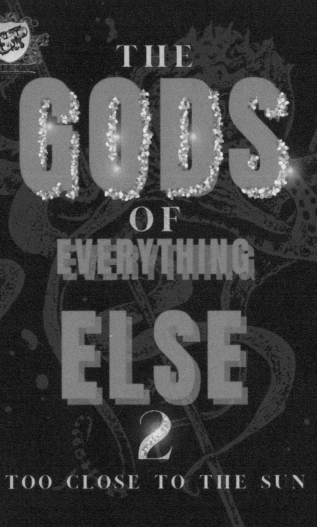

THE GODS OF EVERYTHING ELSE 2

TOO CLOSE TO THE SUN

T. STYLES

NATIONAL BESTSELLING AUTHOR

By T. Styles

ARE YOU ON OUR EMAIL LIST?

SIGN UP ON OUR WEBSITE

www.thecartelpublications.com

OR TEXT THE WORD: CARTELBOOKS

TO 22828

FOR PRIZES, CONTESTS, ETC.

4   **By T. Styles**

THE GOD'S OF EVERYTHING ELSE 2: TOO CLOSE TO THE SUN

By

T. STYLES

PUBLISHER'S NOTE:
This book is a work of fiction. Names,
characters, businesses,
Organizations, places, events and incidents
are the product of the
Author's imagination or are used fictionally.
Any resemblance of
Actual persons, living or dead, events, or
locales are entirely coincidental.

Library of Congress Control Number: 2022905159

ISBN 10: 1948373823

ISBN 13: 978-1948373821

Cover Design: BOOK SLUT CHICK

First Edition

Printed in the United States of America

By T. Styles

What Up Famo,

I'm not even about to do a whole lot of talking in this letter because after what I just finished reading, I don't want to hold you back from reading it any longer.

All I can say is Ace, Ace, Ace...This installment of the series ranks VERY HIGH. Easily top 5 for me. I can't wait to hear how you guys feel. Y'all let me know after you finish. **Toy S. Styles** is a writing master!!!

With that being said, keeping in line with tradition, we want to give respect to a vet, new trailblazer paving the way or pay homage to a favorite. In this novel, we would like to recognize:

James Clear

James Clear is the author of the phenomenal and life changing book, *Atomic Habits*. This book teaches you how to reach the goals the want by shifting your habits. If you want to change your focus to accomplish goals that may seem out of reach, check out this book.

Aight...Get to it! I promise you will not look up until this book is done!

Holla!
Charisse "C. Wash" Washington
Vice President
The Cartel Publications
www.thecartelpublications.com
www.facebook.com/publishercwash
Instagram: Publishercwash
www.twitter.com/cartelbooks
www.facebook.com/cartelpublications
www.theelitewritersacademy.com
Follow us on Instagram: Cartelpublications
#CartelPublications
#UrbanFiction
#PrayForCece
#JamesClear

#THEGODSOFEVERYTHINGELSE2

Dedication

To every T. Styles' Twisted Baby (My Readers)
who has ever read my work, sent me a message,
or created a review, I am eternally grateful for
your undying loyalty after so many years.

I do this for you.

Still.

- T. Styles

By T. Styles

PROLOGUE

The house was a fucking disgrace...

The man in charge of protecting Banks no longer manned the door.

He fled.

Mason Louisville, Walid, Spacey and Joey Wales, couldn't believe their eyes as they took in the mixture of luxury and despair that plagued the familiar place. It looked as if a tornado whipped through the lavish halls of Banks' US mansion with the sole intent of destruction.

Damn...

Their hearts pounded as they continued down the corridors. It didn't help that nature yelled at them from the night sky in the form of thunder and rain that pounded on the estate.

"What do you think is going on?" Spacey whispered as he kicked away the bottom part of a framed Van Goh painting worth over 15 million dollars before it met its demise. "You don't think pops...is hurt do you?"

Mason was too afraid to give his honest opinion. Just the mention of Banks meeting his demise had him wanting to dredge up the darkness he placed at bay many years ago, to make room for his older age.

But unless he laid eyes on his friend within the next minute or two it would be hard not to consider murder in the first, second and third.

"I don't know." They walked around a pile of crystal glass huddled on the floor like mounds of sand. "But make sure you all hang behind me just in case." He tapped his hip to make sure the handle of a familiar friend was nestled in its place.

Of course the weapon was loaded and ready.

The thing was, however, they were all grown men no longer in need of protection. And these days, with the exception of Walid, they were also licensed gun carriers. With that said, they kept their legal shit at home to make room for their street pieces.

No trace.

No case.

Kicking past broken vases and furniture which was splintered wide due to blunt force, they finally happened upon Banks' office. The door was slightly ajar, and all could feel someone menacing was inside.

By T. Styles

Sliding his revolver from his hip, Mason looked behind him and placed a finger over his lips. "Shhhhhh."

Each of the Wales men had their fingers on the triggers of their own pieces and as for now, the barrels hung low.

They were ready for war.

Shoving the door with the muzzle of his revolver, they were shocked to see who was inside.

It was Ace Wales.

He was sitting behind Banks' desk with his feet propped on his paperwork. His face was recently bruised and he looked like he'd been fighting and had gotten whipped *something good*. Since it was raining outside, mud splatters covered some of the documents due to his shoes, and there was a look of satisfaction upon his face that made Spacey want to choke him out.

All lowered their weapons and tucked them back in place but Spacey.

"What you doing in here?" Walid spoke, stepping up from the pack.

"Hey, brother." His curly hair mostly covered his eyes, but the twinkling still shined through.

"I asked you a question." Walid scratched the row between his two French braids to the back. "What you doing sitting in father's chair?"

"I heard you." He uncrossed his legs and recrossed them again, splattering mud on more papers. "But if we going to have a conversation this has to go two ways, wouldn't you agree?"

"You's about a dumb ass little nigga." Spacey said.

Ace placed his feet on the floor and clasped his hands in front of him on the desk, as if he was preparing to negotiate a major deal.

Maybe he was.

Ignoring Spacey all together, he said, "Walid, I'm waiting on my answer."

"You didn't ask me anything."

"Not today." He whipped some curls out of his eyes. They dropped back in place like thick curtains. "But you know what I want to know don't you?"

"Nigga, where is pops?" Spacey questioned no longer being able to handle his level of disrespect. It was also widely known that he didn't care for him in any shape, form, or fashion. Since he was a little kid he thought he was spoiled and had an ego complex so big there wasn't room left for another

16

Wales to survive. "Now ain't nobody come here to see you. Where is pops?"

The barrel of his gun moved on every word and so Mason had to tap him. "Put it up."

"But I don't trust his–."

"Now!" Mason said heavily. When Spacey didn't move quick enough he said, "That's still my son." He pointed a stiff finger in his chest. "And he's still your brother."

Ace grinned.

Spacey tucked the weapon. But he was hoping for an "accidental discharge" if he was being totally honest.

"I know where he is." Ace nodded. "And maybe, depending upon how this conversation goes I'll–"

Just then Walid broke further away from his family and tried to charge him. Again, Mason stopped him with a hand to the chest. Who knows what massacre would have presented itself between the brothers had he not halted his motion.

"Listen, Ace, it's like this...you wanted out." Joey spoke. "We gave you out." He threw both hands up. "Even though you did some shit to all of us, that on the street would've had us drinking to your bones. So why you bothering us now?"

"Except y'all never really let me go. Did you?" He glared.

"It's 'cause you foul, nigga!" Spacey interrupted. "If I had shit my way we wouldn't be even talking right now."

"Then say less, bitch," Ace responded.

"What, little ni–."

Joey stopped Spacey from advancing.

"Son, you've been moving against what I stand for and what Banks stands for too." Mason interrupted. "At the end of the day it's not the Lou or Wales Way."

"I'm so sick of hearing about the Wales Way. Y'all act like y'all some gangsters or something."

Mason chuckled.

Joey and Spacey grinned sinisterly.

The boy had limited knowledge on who the Louisville's and the Wales were before he entered the earth by way of Jersey's cooch. And as a result, his lack of knowledge made him speak ignorantly about things he didn't know. The beach life made him feel as if the street life never existed for the Baltimore natives. And so, he was pressing his luck.

"I'm getting tired." Mason said loudly.

"I know, pops."

"If you really knew, you would not be playing this game."

"Why would I stop the games when I finally see how shit works? Had you let me go the way I wanted none of this would have happened."

"That's the only thing I agree with you on," Spacey said. "Should've let your ass rot in that home for boys."

"If you won't let me out the castle, I'll just blow the bitch up instead."

Walid glared.

Had the others not been in the room, he was certain he would have had his hands around his twin brother's neck. But there was no use in trying to go against the elders. He would have his personal time with Ace soon, if he didn't let on where Banks was before night's end.

"Pops, do you remember the Greek story you told me of Icarus?"

Silence.

"I'll take your lack of answering as a yes." He laughed once and rose, while standing next to the window which lit up in shades of light blue off dark purple every time thunder clapped the sky. "In the story you told me about the boy who flew too close to the sun due to flying with wings made of wax."

"Get to your point."

"Well, your story has a flaw."

"Y'all feeling this nigga?" Spacey said, wondering why he hadn't been knocked on the head and bagged already.

"Chill," Joey whispered.

"Had Daedalus, Icarus' father, not made trash wings, they both would have survived. And the sun would not have liquified the wings."

"You sound dumb, son. Where is Banks?"

"But you're right about comparing me with Icarus though." He pointed at him, refusing to stop his frame of thought. "Except it wasn't my fault things got as bad as they are right now in our family, as everybody likes to put on. And it wasn't Icarus' fault they both died either. Just like with my life, everything that I fucking am and do is because of father. He's the villain not me."

"Once again you speak about things you don't know." Mason responded. "I never told you they both died, son."

Ace blinked.

"Just Icarus. And if you aren't careful, even though you carry my blood in your veins, you will too."

"Is that a threat?"

By T. Styles

"Do you want it to be?" Spacey pleaded.

Ace giggled.

"Where is father?" Walid pressed a bit harder.

"Before I tell you where he is, let me give you my stance on everything. You're going to have your opinions anyway but at least you'll hear where I'm coming from."

"Nobody cares." Joey said, clapping with each word.

"You see that's the problem." He beat his chest once. "It was always Walid!" He pointed at him. "Always everybody else. Nobody ever gave a fuck about me." He paused when he felt himself getting too emotional. Lowering his head, he took a deep breath and looked at each of them. "You better learn to try to understand me. Because I will tear the rest of Wales and Lou legacy down, I swear to God."

Mason, Spacey and Joey sighed.

"These are the things that led to father being no more..." Ace continued.

Mason's heart rocked.

And everyone looked at one another in complete fear.

"Are you saying that he's dead?" Mason felt dizzy.

He laughed, sat in the chair, and slammed his feet back on the desk. "Once upon a time..."

CHAPTER ONE
ACE
6 MONTHS EARLIER
"They are non-negotiable."

A ce and Arbella's new crib was spectacular.

Finally feeling like he was away from Banks' hand, Ace dipped into the funds he had stolen from him small portion after small portion and splurged on a luxury penthouse apartment in the suburbs of Silver Spring, Maryland.

White on white was the concept with everything else, including the paintings on the walls, being accented in gold. Ace gave her access to the banking account and full ability to buy whatever she needed to make their place feel like home.

After all, it was a celebration!

It took months and a lot of throwing Banks' men off his trail and after what seemed like forever, they left the trash apartment and moved under the cover of night to what matched his fly. And to be sure that no one would learn his whereabouts the new apartment was in Arbella's name.

Ace had it all worked out.

He had outsmarted the king.

They were bringing in their last boxes with the help of a moving crew and the young couple was looking forward to doing *them* in the bedroom. It was hard for Ace to resist too because Arbella looked stunning in her peach jumper with her natural black hair tossed on the top of her head in what he called a sex bun. She managed to keep it in place too, with a 14-karat gold writing pen that she used to record every task that had to be done for them to live in comfort.

Arbella was good with the details. And this afforded Ace to do what he wanted with his free time.

Floss.

After sitting a box on the kitchen counter full of utensils, Ace walked past the mirror over the sink and a seat of rage riled up in his stomach as he took in his reflection.

Despite still possessing most of his natural good looks, his face, which had been lacerated multiple times by her ex-boyfriend Lance Laurent, and several other places showcased raised scars that would never disappear. Strangers got the impression that although he was still attractive, that the disfigurement made him sinister.

Unable to stand his own likeness, he readjusted his gaze and unpacked a few items and put them anywhere he could tuck them.

No worries.

Arbella would organize the shit later.

He just wanted to appear helpful so she could suck his dick in the shower, like she knew he loved, that evening.

"Where do you want this box, sir?" The mover questioned entering the penthouse.

"Place it over on the side." Ace pointed as he grabbed a bunch of spoons and tossed them in a cabinet any old kind of way. "Next to the couch."

"But make sure you put it on the plastic." Arbella directed. "I don't want the white carpet destroyed."

"Yeah, whatever she just said." Ace grabbed a box with his sneaks and walked them into his bedroom.

When he came back he noticed the moving man was talking to Arbella too closely.

Rage, something he knew good enough to be a close friend, presented itself in his body. First his stomach tingled. Then his heart kicked at his chest cavity. Finally his temples throbbed and before he could stop himself he said, "My nigga, are you finished or are you done?"

Both Arbella and the Moving Man caught all his heat.

"Oh, yes." He spoke. "I was just commenting about how nice this crib is." He looked up at the vaulted ceiling and back at him. "A friend of mine got–."

"I don't need you commenting on how nice my shit is." He shrugged repeatedly. "I already know." He stepped closer. "And I also don't need you talking to my bitch about your life because she ain't about to be a part of it." He pointed at his steel toe boots. "Now take your moving blankets and get the fuck up out my shit."

"I didn't mean any disrespect."

"And yet you disrespected all the same." Over the shoulder pointing. "Now bounce."

It was a long walk to the door, but the Moving Man made it out with his life.

When he was gone Ace walked up to her where suddenly she was extra interested in the clipboard in her hand.

He stood over top of her...breathing heavily.

He removed the writing pen from her hair and her locks fell alongside her shoulders. She swept them back to get strands out of her face.

Clearing her throat she said, "So all we have to do now is–"

"What I tell you about speaking to other dudes?"

She laughed. "Ace, cut it out."

He breathed heavier.

"Wait, you were serious about that list?"

"Am I tripping, or did I give you my rules?"

"You did but..."

"They are non-negotiable."

"Ace, all I was doing was speaking to him about one of his friends. I didn't mean anything by it and neither did he. I think you're taking this a little too–"

"Do you need me to recite the rules again or nah?"

A deep breath filled her chest. "No." She exhaled. "I got it." She shook her head. "I just wish if you were going to place these types of rules upon me that you would at least make me your wife."

If you wanted to back him away, those were the magic words. Because even though he was sure she was the one, he was enjoying the attention he got from finally living away from the island.

In his American travels, women looked at him and went out of their way to speak. And he enjoyed the possibility of fucking a Baltimore/DC bred dime in the future. So getting married at the current, wasn't on his list of priorities.

Besides, he had her already.

It was always about the new.

"Drop it." He walked away.

"Why, Ace? You push these rules on me and I need more to feel secure."

"Which I explained to you was a possibility before you ever became mine."

"I get that. But you promised you would marry me. It was your idea. You said because you were alone. And if something ever happened to you, because of your family, I would need to be in a position to make decisions." She felt emboldened so it was she who stepped closer this time. "So, either you want me to ride with you or you don't. But you can't have it both ways."

He was just about to go a little further when the doorbell rang. "Who's that?"

Her eyes widened.

Outside of the moving men, no one should have their address, but her eyes said differently.

"Who is it, Arbella?"

"I may have told my father where we live just in case."

"Why the fuck would you do that?"

"Please try to get along with him."

"Get along?" He roared. "Let me be clear, this will be the first and last time that man will ever be allowed in my house."

DING DONG.

"Baby, please don't—."

"Are we clear?"

"Ace..."

"Tell me you understand, Arbella."

"Yes, but my father has a lot of connections, Ace. And with the trouble you get into you may need to remember that in case you're ever in a bind."

"He will never be allowed in here again. Ever! I will die before I call on him."

Ace walked away as she trudged towards the door.

Within a few seconds her father entered.

The moment he saw Ace his face lit up. To say that he considered him the plug to a fortune was an understatement. Mr. Valentine really believed that with Ace being the son of a billionaire that within time his bank account would swell too.

His biggest pride in life was having a daughter so fine, she attracted money bags.

"Hello, baby." Mr. Valentine said, planting a quick kiss on her face while his eyes rested on the boy king.

The recessed lighting shined on his chocolate skin and bald head. And his brows were as bushy as ever which made it slightly difficult to see his eyes.

"This is a beautiful apartment." He said in a deep voice that rolled like thunder.

"Penthouse." Ace corrected.

"I mean penthouse." He glided around Arbella and slid toward Ace as if he were on skates. "You've done well for my daughter. At first I wasn't sure but now I'm certain she made the right decision."

"Listen, I didn't ask you to come over."

"I don't follow."

"Why are you in my face?"

Mr. Valentine cleared his throat. "I know somewhere along the line I rubbed you the wrong way. But I'm hoping we can get past that now."

"Dad, he will learn to like you. He's just concerned that–"

"I'm talking to him." Mr. Valentine said, interrupting her. "Now let the man speak."

Ace was enraged. But for the moment he chose to take a different route since he was on his dick. "I heard you were close to Lance, her ex."

"At one point that was true."

"Where is he? I'm still looking for him."

"No need to worry about him. Your father and his people scared him straight. He won't be a bother."

"Where is he?" Ace pressed him like a hot iron.

Mr. Valentine shuffled a little. "Actually no one has been able to find him. Not since you and your father returned." He laughed. "Like I said, I guess the Wales successfully scared him and his father Satchel away. He's just some rich kid unaware of how to act in a war."

"You were in hiding for a bit too." Ace continued.

Silence.

"Listen, just so you know, I'm not on good terms with my father." Ace continued. "So, anything that you think you're going to get by sucking my dick, is a waste of time. Besides, I have your daughter to do that."

Ace had a reason for being vile.

He wanted to see if he cared about Arbella. He wanted to detect any glance that disrespect for his child would cause problems.

Mr. Valentine didn't budge.

Because Mr. Valentine didn't care.

"Ace, please don't talk to my father like that. It's so–."

"Sweetheart, be quiet." Mr. Valentine said. "Men are talking. How many times must I tell you that?"

Ace had enough.

"You know what, get out of my fucking house." He said pointing over his shoulder.

Mr. Valentine was shocked because Lance never defended Arbella before, so why should he? In fact, Lance seemed to enjoy the displays of putting Arbella in her place.

Ace felt differently.

"Why do you want me to leave? I didn't mean to cause trouble. But she must learn to respect men when they are talking. She's just like her mother in that aspect."

By T. Styles

"The thing is you're still talking to me after I told you to bounce. I won't say it again though."

He nodded and took a deep breath. "One of these days you are going to realize how much you need me. And when you do, I'll forget about all of this." He kissed Arbella on the cheek and walked out the door.

She moved closer. "I know you don't like him. But he's still my father and he's very important to me."

"That's the only reason he's still alive." He took a deep breath. "But like I said, he is never allowed in here again. And the relationship you had with him is over. Now tell me you understand."

Silence.

"Arbella, tell me what I want to hear."

"It's done."

He kissed her lips. "Now hurry up. I need you to wrap them lips around my dick."

CHAPTER TWO
WALID
"Running around the streets of America is out."

Walid and Aliyah were fucking face first.

As she sat on top of his lap, he gripped her right and left cheek and pressed upward into her gushiness. Feeling good, her head dropped back and he kissed her neck, before running his wet tongue around her nipples.

She tasted so sweet.

And was always so wet, that he wondered due to the number of times they made love, why she hadn't run dry.

When her head lowered and they looked into each other's eyes, her hair clinging to the sides of her face, the tingling sensation they experienced intensified. Their love was uncommon, especially since at one point in time she belonged to his twin.

And every moment they fucked, the fact that their love story was almost never born, made their passion higher.

"Hmmmm, Walid, I...I love you." She said scratching at his back.

When she expressed her feelings, it was hard not releasing his load, but he wanted to try. "Talking like that is the reason I'm knee deep in this pussy now."

Suddenly her body pushed up and down in the rhythm of each stroke and before long, she exploded over his dick. This gave him full permission to spring his cream into her body, until she safeguarded each drop.

When they were done, she sat up in bed yoga style and created a mound of covers to hide her breasts and in between her legs in case someone opened the door per usual, in Banks' US estate.

As her breathing settled to normal, a weird smile rested on her face that he was all too familiar with. "What do you want, Aliyah?"

He tugged at the drawer by his bed and pulled out a pipe. Lately he took a liking to the sweet taste and smell, after walking into a shop to get some cigars with Spacey one day. It was a strange habit for such a young man and in some ways, since most felt like he'd been here in a past life, it also fit.

"Before you say no, I have a babysitter." She started.

He inhaled and held the smoke. The free hand rested on his softening dick. Releasing smoke into the air he said, "Aliyah what do you want?"

"To see Baltimore city. I...I heard of so many nice restaurants and places we could go on the water that it would make–"

He pulled and exhaled again. "We not here on vacation."

She frowned. "I get that but–."

"I don't think you do though. The moment my father finishes his business I want to go back home. So all this shit you trying to do, with running around the streets of America is out."

"Walid, you're speaking to me as if I'm a child."

"Never said you were. But looking at the smile on your face it makes me think that you don't take things seriously." He placed the pipe on the holder and eased off the bed. Next he walked to the corner and grabbed his burgundy robe off the stand.

"We aren't done talking."

"I think we are."

"Okay...okay let's do this." She said excitedly.

He shook his head, already feeling a press coming on.

"Would you agree that we are here for the next few months no matter what?"

36   **By T. Styles**

He sighed and dragged his hand down his face.

"Walid, the least you can do is answer the question."

"You're asking me what's obvious."

"True. But roll with me anyway."

"Yes, I agree we here no matter what."

"And since we're here no matter what, we might as well enjoy ourselves. Or would you prefer to be miserable?"

Walid had opinions on his mental state, and he would keep them to himself. But when he finished kicking it with his wife, son, father, brothers and even the young Louisville clan, depression kept him company.

Because at the end of the day he was growing tired of not being in Belize. Almost every day he would call Morgan, his caregiver, to see how things were on Wales Island. Although her health was failing more than ever, he enjoyed talking to her about how peaceful things were back home.

And he longed to return, even if it was just he, his wife and son.

So staying in Baltimore when it didn't compare in his opinion was beyond annoying.

"I would prefer to be home. But to answer your question, if my only options are misery and happiness I would go with happiness."

"Exactly!" She said, clapping her hands together as if she had finally gotten through to him. The sheets dropped exposing her breasts. "I would go with happiness too."

"Aliyah...I'm growing annoyed. What's your point?"

"Okay, okay, so I was thinking that maybe I could go on the town with Joey's wife while–"

"What is it with you two lately? You spend every moment on the phone with her. Whenever she comes over, y'all post up in the dining room for hours. What is the connection?"

She shrugged. "I don't know. She gets me."

"And what exactly are y'all planning to do if I say yes?"

She walked over to him in the nude. He could still smell the slight but pleasant odor of their sexual encounter. Kissing him on the lips she said, "I'm getting my nails and toes done and maybe buy a few outfits followed by dinner. After that I'll return home and do whatever you want. I'll even sleep with your dick in my mouth the way you like it."

"If I say no, you'll do that anyway."

"Please, Walid. You have to learn to trust me. Like I trust you." She paused. "We have never held secrets from each other. So why would we start now?"

That statement caused guilt to rile up in his soul.

He knew he harbored many things she didn't know. For starters, he slept with Arbella under the guise of being Ace to get information on his whereabouts when Lance snatched him some months back.

To make it worse, many years ago he accidently killed her father in a vehicle accident, something she didn't know.

He looked at her for a bit long and then took a deep breath. To be honest she was kind of annoying him so perhaps he could get a little peace with her gone, even if only for a few hours.

"Okay."

She jumped on him, and her legs straddled his waist. Because she was completely naked, he stiffened immediately and used the opportunity to go back inside of her pussy. It didn't take him long to bust, and once again she was filled with his cream.

"Thank you." She kissed his lips.

"For what part?"

"The dick, and your trust." She grabbed her robe and ran down the hallway to tell Sydney the good news.

He was just about to get something to eat when Blakeslee entered.

The moment he saw her, his dick shriveled up, he fixed his robe and sighed.

She had a way of annoying him that was eerily similar to Ace. And since she was Ace's biggest fan it was easy to understand why.

"What do you want?" He walked to the bed, grabbed his pipe, and plopped down.

"The Triad is looking for you."

"What I tell you about calling them that?"

"That's the name they gave themselves. Blame them, not me."

The Triad consisted of 15-year-old Patrick, who was Mason's grandson, 14-year-old Bolt, who was Mason's son and 16-year-old Riot, who was Spacey's only child.

Only Riot was not bound to him in blood.

"Well, what do they want? And why they send you?"

"Because I was coming this way."

By T. Styles

"Well I'm busy so I'll get up with them in a minute."

"I saw Aliyah leave." She batted her eyes. "You two look sooooo happy."

"And?" He shrugged and pulled on his pipe.

"Well, it's just that your other brother would like to be happy too."

"I got many brothers."

"I'm talking about Ace."

"Blakeslee, what the fuck Ace got to do with me?"

"He wonders when you are going to return his calls. If you ask me, you're acting very petty when whatever is going on with him and father has nothing to do with you."

"First of all, if father found out you're still talking to him, you could be in a heap of trouble."

"Trouble, trouble, I love it on the double."

"You sound stupid when you say that shit." He pulled. Puffed. And smoke filled the air.

She glared. "Nah, you know what's stupid?"

"I'm listening."

"The fact that you fucked Arbella and Aliyah doesn't know. Neither does Ace for now." She giggled. "Of course, that all could change."

Walid felt faint.

Dropping his pipe, he rushed past her and closed the door. Grabbing her by the shoulders he said, "What did you just say?"

"You smell like pussy and dick."

"What did you say about Arbella?" He said more forcibly.

"I said, I know you slept with Arbella."

"You don't know what you're talking about. And if I were you, I would be careful."

"But I do know what I'm saying. And the longer you spend not speaking to your brother it makes me wonder if Aliyah will still think you're the greatest guy on Earth if she knew the truth. Sure hope I don't have to tell her." She blew a kiss.

He took his hand and mushed her lips and face.

"Mmmmm," She inhaled. "I got a good smell of her now. Maybe if Ace finds out she's so sweet, he will like the scent of Aliyah too. You know, for revenge and all." With that she giggled and walked out the door.

By T. Styles

CHAPTER THREE
SPACEY
"Wait, so I don't understand pain?"

S pacey scratched his scruffy beard as he walked down Banks' hallway toward the room Minnesota Wales occupied in the estate. When he reached the door he took a deep breath and knocked softly.

"Go away." She said from the other side.

His forehead leaned against the door. "You know I can't do that."

"Please, Spacey."

"I'm coming inside."

He entered the room and the first thing that hit him was the staleness in the air. When he looked at the bed, he saw her huddled up with so many sheets it was difficult to find where her body began or ended. On every available surface, flowers sat which due to dying, carried a sweet stench reminiscent of a funeral.

First he opened the window, to cleanse the air. Then he shut the door, sat on the edge of the bed, and looked outward at the open window. The garden, the basketball court and the land surrounding the estate was spectacular.

"Minnesota, how much longer?"

"My husband was just murdered, Spacey. I mean, why would you ask me something like that anyway?"

"I'm not saying how long you will grieve. I'm asking how much longer will you stay in this room and away from the people who care about you? You have to pull yourself together."

Suddenly the mound in the center of the bed moved and her head peeked out as if she were a baby chicken hatching from an egg. Her uncombed hair was all over her face and her eyes were dark and puffy.

"You could never understand what I'm experiencing right now. So why would you feel it was within your right to speak on it?"

He glared. "Wait, so I don't understand pain?"

"It's different."

"How is it different? We lost our mother. We lost Harris. And when great-grandmother locked us away in that attic, I felt as if the world had abandoned us too. I still feel that shit."

"I can't do this right now."

By T. Styles

"And even though you and I were together..." he continued. "There were many times when I felt if you wanted you could leave me alone. Trust me, I know pain."

"I never left you, Spacey."

"I know you didn't. And I'm not leaving you now." He positioned his body to look at her. "All I'm asking is that you let us help you. Let me help you take a shower. Make you a meal. Let me show you how much I love you. It's all I want, Minnesota. Can you do that for me? Please."

"You never liked Zercy. And deep in your heart, I know you're glad he's gone. Secretly hoping you could fuck me again, huh?" She took a deep breath and hid herself back under the mounds. "Let yourself out, Spacey. I won't tell you again."

"Okay."

He walked away feeling more guilty than ever.

The problem was not that she threw him out, but that what she said was true. On many occasions, he celebrated Zercy's death.

And he was glad he was gone.

THE TRIAD

The Triad was in the workout room lifting.

Just like his father back in the day, Patrick whose 15-year-old muscled physique was about to prove that he could bench press 200. While 14-year-old Bolt spotted him, he was just about to push to accept the barbell when 16-year-old Riot stepped on his toe.

"Damn, white boy!"

Because Riot had taken most of his features from the Caucasian side of the family, his silky black hair and extra light skin made it next to impossible to identify his African American heritage. This feature caused The Triad to hand him a nickname, that he wasn't all the way feeling.

White Boy.

"Sorry...I was just trying to film it." He said, holding the video camera, which he was allowed to have although cell phones for the youngins were still banned.

"Well film it the fuck back there."

By T. Styles

"I'm ready," Patrick said, as Bolt raised the bar and held it over his head. True to life, Patrick pushed up and down five times before the barbell came slamming down on the rack.

The Triad went off when he was done. Hand slaps, hugs, and cheers as if he'd won a race. They were definitely close, and the bond they experienced grew more intense in isolation.

"You next, Bolt," Patrick said pointing, while dabbing his face with a towel.

He frowned. "I never said I could do it."

"Yeah, but you need it more than us," Riot added.

"Why?"

"For starters you a little too sweet." Patrick said. "If you gonna be in our family, you gotta be strong. It's the Wales and Lou way."

"But you not a Wales though." Bolt added.

"We still a part of this family though." Patrick said. "Uncle Banks said so himself."

"And I'm his grandson soooo." Riot grinned.

"I'm not even sure how much longer this family gonna last," Bolt admitted.

"Why you say that?" Patrick spoke.

"With Ace being gone, and not wanting to come home, maybe our family done all the way around." Bolt continued.

"Nah, we not," Walid said entering the gym.

He dapped up each of them as they happily gave him love. Just like with Blakeslee, they all had a favorite twin, and Walid was it for The Triad.

Moving toward the bench he said, "Rack 'em up, little neph."

"It's already 200 on it." Riot responded.

"Fuck I look like? Y'all young asses? Add 200 more."

Riot excitedly did as he was told, once done, Riot filmed the entire thing on his camera.

"And just so y'all know, whether Ace comes back or not, we still family. We ain't about to let one nigga break our bond. Y'all just look out for each other and before you know it we will be back home. That's on God."

With that Walid pushed the weights in the air.

And The Triad went wild.

CHAPTER FOUR
BANKS
"If you're late again we're done."

Even the boardroom lights looked good on the Wales' and the Lou.

All of them were freshly dressed and groomed and just one glance would make it clear they came from money.

Banks was sitting at the head of the table, in one of the many buildings he owned in Baltimore, Maryland. Mason was at his side along with Spacey and Joey, his sons, who more resembled goons than businessmen.

Every now and then Banks would look down at his phone, and an expression of dissatisfaction would wash over him.

And Mason noticed it all.

He always noticed his moods and temperaments, keeping them in his mind like the entries of a diary.

"I think you should let him be." Mason said on the wave of a long breath. "Like really leave that little nigga 'lone."

Banks tucked his phone in his pocket and leaned back in his chair. "I don't know what you're talking about."

"Except you do though."

"Leave it, Mason." Joey said, leaning forward to look at him. "He ain't about to let his youngest son be out on his own and we all know it."

"But I won't leave it. First of all, he's my son too."

"Yuck," Joey said.

"There he goes being weird again," Spacey spoke, hating how Mason kept reminding everybody that two men essentially had children together.

"It ain't being weird. Because we all know the reason we're still in America is in the hopes that Ace will come around. But the boy ain't built to fall in line." Mason focused on Banks. "The reality is this, this may be the first time in life you won't get what you want, Banks."

"Do you really think God created a world where I don't get everything I desire?"

Joey laughed.

"Age has made you worse."

Before Banks gave him a piece of his mind Kordell Fuego entered.

By T. Styles

A few months back when Banks and Mason were stranded in Mexico it was he and his men who helped him escape the wicked and vicious Nicolas who was set on killing them both. And as payment, Kordell the drug dealer wanted to be Kordell the businessman.

He wanted what Banks had.

He wanted out of the game.

He needed the billionaire's help.

It didn't appear like it to some, but they had a lot in common. Because Kordell was also from Baltimore. And just like so many others, he fell in love with Mexico and made his mark. But unlike many, he was one of the quietest and powerful drug dealers still operating in the US. But that was changing and people were starting to take notice. And notice would bring only two things...murder or police.

At the end of the day, if Kordell was a cat, he would be on his ninth life.

Kordell, with his chocolate skin and neat dreads with rings running down his back, walked closer to the table with two Mexican men on the left and right.

"I don't know what Banks said to you, but we don't do the late shit." Mason spoke.

Kordell and his men took their seats.

He snickered. "What is it with you always feeling the need to speak up for Banks? He can defend himself."

"This guy." Joey said, shaking his head in irritation. He met the man for two minutes and already didn't like him.

"So let me make it clear for you." Banks spoke. "If you're late again we're done."

Mason smiled.

Spacey grinned.

Joey sat back.

"No need to do all that. We here for business, so let's do business."

Banks looked over at Joey who stood up and handed him a report along with the two men at Kordell's side. When he was done he reclaimed his seat closer to his father.

"This is the direction I think you should go." Banks said as he and his crew all glanced down at the documents in front of them.

Mason, Joey nor Spacey cared less about Kordell's plan. But they played along for the optics and all.

Kordell looked at the document and frowned. "What is this?"

By T. Styles

"It's your new business venture."

He shook his head. "I mean I need some help but I also had some ideas of my own."

"Let me get this straight, you want to be like my pops but you want to do the same hood nigga shit you accustomed?" Joey spoke. "Is that what you're saying? Because I'm asking for a friend."

"That's what it sounds like to me," Spacey cosigned.

Kordell sat back. "It's not that but I was thinking of opening a slew of strip clubs in the city so I can go legit and have fun too."

Banks wanted to grab what was left of his time and bounce. In the moment, for Kordell to have survived in the game as long as he did undetected had Banks shocked because he sounded stupid.

"Have you ever met a billionaire who sold titties?" Banks asked.

"Before Banks, have you met a billionaire period?" Mason added.

Kordell glared. "You didn't even listen to my plan."

"Because that's not what this is about. You solicited my help 'cause–"

"No, you solicited he." The Mexican man at his right said while pointing down at the table.

Banks sighed. "I didn't solicit shit. I called on him for help, and he responded. I was perfectly willing to pay his fee had he named a price. But he didn't. He wanted financial advice which was a smart move." He pointed at the table. "But this is what it's about."

"You with it or not?" Joey asked.

"So no strip clubs, huh?"

"Nah." Mason said, shaking his head slowly.

He bit his lip and looked down at the paper. "So what is this anyway?"

"I have in front of you a list of the most talented app creators in the world. Not just the United States but internationally. If you want to be a billionaire, you have to go digital. NFT's, cryptocurrency and shit of that nature. That's how you wash your money."

"But I don't know nothing about this shit."

"Exactly. That's why you hired me."

Suddenly Banks' phone rang. When he saw who it was, he glared. "Give me a second." He stood up and took the call in the corner of the office standing next to the window. "What, Blakeslee?"

"Can I go outside?" She asked from the home phone.

"Are you stupid?"

"Father!"

"Why do I have to keep telling you the same thing over and over? This isn't a vacation or retreat. Once we do what we came to do we're gone."

"But Aliyah got to go out with Sydney."

Banks hung up.

He had no time for it even though he was aware that he should probably give more attention to his youngest daughter. He was just about to rejoin the table when suddenly two of his men entered.

Their entry in and of itself was legit because Banks had so much security on the outside of the boardroom that if you weren't supposed to be there you weren't getting in.

He rushed toward them. "What is it?"

"Ace moved from the first apartment."

His brows lowered. "How do you know?"

Spacey, Joey and Mason walked behind him and all waited for the answer. Meanwhile Kordell sat over at the table heated as fuck.

"Because the landlady we paid to keep us informed said when she went into the apartment like you requested each night, this time all of his things were gone."

Banks stepped closer. "Where is he?"

Silence.

"Answer the question, nigga!" Spacey yelled.

"We don't know."

"So you coming to my meeting to interrupt me with nothing but bad news?"

"Sir, I am so sorry. But I promise you–"

Banks walked away and toward the exit.

"What's going on?" Kordell yelled from the table.

"Pick one of the options I listed and I'll contact you when it's time."

"Don't forget you owe me! I don't do well when I don't get what I'm due."

"Are you threatening my father?" Spacey asked.

Suddenly the boardroom was filled with 10 men, all gentlemen, but each one with fingertips hovering over the humps on their hips.

"No. Just saying."

"Look over the list." Banks continued. "Or not. Either way I don't give a fuck."

He and his men stormed out.

CHAPTER FIVE
BLAKESLEE
"Because you scared of my daddy."

Blakeslee sat in the back of the house watching a game of basketball with The Triad take place.

Banks had the court built along with the gate surrounding the estate, to prevent the dangerous inertia he was sure the youngest of the family experienced while living in America. Once again, due to fear, he did all he could to prevent them from escaping and getting into trouble.

She was bored to death and was annoyed at The Triad because prior to being in America, they would get into mischief together on their island and sometimes at sea. Now with age and time, they didn't find a place for her in their lives.

She needed Ace.

And she needed him badly.

"How much longer are y'all going to play that stupid game?" She said as they continued to bounce the ball up and down the court. Their young bodies glistening with sweat under the sun.

They ignored her on purpose.

She was somewhat embarrassed, and it grew worse when she saw the security guards Banks hired laughing at her need to be seen on the sidelines. Clearing her throat and standing up she yelled, "I said how much longer are y'all gonna be?"

"Why?" Riot shouted; his long hair braided toward the back like Walid. "You see we busy and shit."

"Shut up, White Boy. You just trying to be tough in front of them."

"Go bang your head into a closet door!" Bolt yelled as he shot and missed. "You messing us up."

Frustrated as all get out, she stormed into the house and toward the kitchen. Just like Minnesota when she was younger, she was considered a flight risk. And because of it a guard followed closely behind her at all times. This did nothing but make her angrier and birthed in her many ideas of mischief.

But what could she do?

Grabbing a soda out of the refrigerator she walked toward the living room. Her red painted toes slapped against the marbled floors as she plopped on the sofa.

Her detail was still there, watching from the corner.

58   By T. Styles

"You a freak ain't you?" She asked him.

Silence.

"I could probably do anything I wanted and you would let me. Because you scared of my daddy."

Silence.

"So you just gonna ignore me too?"

Silence.

This is when she decided to fuck with him a bit harder.

Widening her legs, she pushed back her skirt, grabbed the soda bottle, and rubbed it around her middle. He tried to look away but when she began to moan it was difficult.

His reaction made her smile.

"Yeah, you a freak."

"You aren't being a nice girl. That can put you in a bind in the future."

"Trouble, trouble I love it on the double."

"Stupid."

Annoyed with him already, she rose and he remained on her heels.

"I'm going to the bathroom you know?" She walked inside and closed the door. "I could escape from this window and it would be nothing you could do about it!" She yelled at the door.

Giggling her face off, her heart rocked when he entered.

"You want me to do anything for you?" His entire presence filled up the bathroom, which wasn't an easy feat since it was huge. He closed the door behind himself. "Need me to suck on them titties?"

Her heart pounded harder. "You better get out of here before–"

He stepped closer. No air between them. "Before you what? Tell somebody?" He laughed. "Little rich bitches like you think you can do and say what you want and won't nobody call you up on it."

"I'm sorry." She trembled.

"Let me hear you say it louder."

"I'm sorry." She swallowed the lump in her throat.

"That's what the fuck I thought. Now open your mouth."

She did as she was told and he placed his thumb on her tongue, followed by the next finger and then all five.

"You quiet now huh?"

She nodded with a hand in her mouth.

Removing it, he grabbed the back of her head and pressed his dry lips against hers. His palm was so huge it covered her skull completely.

"The next time you play a game like you did out there, with opening your legs so I can see that pussy, I'm gonna have you bent over this bathroom sink and you're going to take every inch of this dick too."

Tears started welling up in her eyes. She had to do something to get her power back.

And what was more powerful than the Wales name?

"And I'll tell my father. Do you hear me?"

He lowered his body and leaned closer to her. "Not if I kill that nigga first. And the Lou's too. Is that what you want?"

She shook her head slowly from left to right.

He snatched the bottle and inhaled the top. "Damn...you smell like piss. Fucking ruined it for me." He laughed and walked out the door.

Embarrassed, she slammed her panties down, flopped on the toilet, and cried while she peed.

CHAPTER SIX
ACE
"I guess he not all you thought he was right?"

This was supposed to be the night of all nights...

The way Ace saw it, shit was going along as planned for the evening. And yet the suit he wore was two sizes too big and made him look like a clown. Had he not been so bent on "showing her the world" she could've helped him make the appropriate selection. After all, on the island he always had a stylist for moments like this. But now, with money at his disposal he was the living embodiment of every gangsta movie he'd ever seen. From *Scarface* to *Paid In Full*, he jammed them all together and looked ridiculous.

Ace helped Arbella in her seat and the *I AM GOD* chain knocked against her temple.

"Ouch!" She stroked it with a few fingers.

"My bad." He sat across from her in the expensive five-star restaurant, sliding the chair loudly across the floor like a child.

"It's okay." She smiled, looked around and rubbed her slightly scratched temple.

62   By T. Styles

When from the floor to ceiling window he saw a derelict eating bread and begging for money, he glared. In his mind he could imagine how poorly he smelled based on his soiled disposition. "You see that shit?" He asked.

She looked over at him from the window. "Yeah, it's sad."

"No it's not! He gotta put his work in like the rest of us."

"But your father is a billionaire. And you have millions."

"So what. I don't feel shit for niggas like that." He flagged the manager over and gave him his spill.

"Right away, sir."

Within two seconds, the derelict was gone.

Arbella was ashamed.

Proud of himself he said, "You like it in here?" He nodded. "Ain't this the best place you've ever been?"

She'd been there ten times. In fact, she, and her friends who she was no longer in contact with at one time were regulars. Due to their beauty, they would sit at the bar and never have to reach in their purse because strangers always picked up the tab.

"It is. I've never heard of this place before." She sipped her water and a small block of ice collided against her top lip. "So you really know how to pick 'em."

His ego grew swollen with each word. "So Lance didn't bring you here either huh?"

She didn't feel like playing the game anymore. After all, she had already lied for his sake. "No, Ace. You are my first."

He wanted more. "I guess he not all you thought he was right?"

"Why do you do that?" She shook her head.

"What you talking about?" He grabbed a piece of bread and dipped it in the warm butter, before taking a bite and dipping it again, mixing his saliva in the condiment which was meant for the table.

"You talk about Lance every five minutes."

He dropped the roll to the floor. "I'm sorry, but do I have to move closer so you can see my fucking face?" He pointed to the scars.

"I didn't mean it that way and you know it."

"I keep asking you about him because when I see him, and I will, he'll be my first kill."

She frowned. "First kill?"

"Trust me." He picked the roll up off the floor, dipped it into the butter and chewed with his mouth open.

As the days went by, Arbella was starting to feel he was exhibiting signs of mental illness or missing his family so terribly he was losing control. "Ace, when you were a kid did you–."

"I'm not a kid." He chewed like a cow.

If one looked at the suit which swallowed up his frame, they couldn't help but think he was a cute little baby boy.

Still, she wanted answers to her question. Was he well or was he unraveling out of control? "Um, did I ever tell you about an aunt in my family?"

He shrugged. "If you did I can't remember."

"Well, she suffered from bipolar disorder and had to get help after jumping in front of a train."

It was true.

"Damn, I remember my father talking about my grandmother. She suffered from bipolar disease too."

Her eyes widened. "Oh, because it's inheritable by 80% or more."

He shrugged again. "Good thing it skipped me then."

Did it though?

"Ace, when are you going to marry me?"

"Why do you keep bringing that shit up? Ain't nobody trying to marry a person who keeps begging and shit."

She sighed and was intent on standing her ground. "When my mother was burned there came a time when it was believed a decision would have to be made to take her off the ventilator or let her survive. Since at the time we thought my father was responsible it was scary to think that he could be in control of her life."

"And this is the dude you want coming around our crib?"

"Ace, listen. Sometimes I don't think you're well. And since it's me and you against the world I want to be there for you when needed. And I'm afraid that if I build a life with you, and if something happens, I won't be able to take care of you. That your father would step in."

"Still, don't you think you're moving a little fast?"

She frowned. "Fast? You were the one who pushed up on me and told me that we had to move quickly with our relationship. Because you didn't know what your father would do."

"I hear all that but–"

66   By T. Styles

"So I need to know it's real."

Ace went silent for a moment and then he took a deep breath. "If all of the bad things didn't happen, with Lance, would you have chosen me or him?"

"I don't understand the question."

Before he could respond the waiter came over and took their requests. Per usual Ace ordered for them both. When the waiter left he grinned proudly.

"What's so funny?" She spoke.

"I bet you he never did that before. Talking about Lance."

"You mean order steak when I wanted chicken?"

Silence.

"I'm starting to feel a type of way, Ace. Like I know you want to be with me but is this a competition or—"

Before she could finish her sentence, three pretty girls in a variety of shades walked up to the table. They were all dressed fashionably and had plastered smiles on their lightly painted faces.

Ace could tell immediately that Arbella knew them and was uncomfortable.

"Arbella, is that you?" The Brownest of them all spoke.

She nodded but her body was tense.

"We been looking everywhere for you, girl."

"You mean tonight?" He spoke, curious about their existence.

The trio looked at him and laughed. "No, not tonight." The Brownest one said sarcastically.

Ace was embarrassed.

And the embarrassment had him wanting to act out.

"Why would you be looking for me?" Arbella questioned.

"Because we didn't know if you knew what's been happening."

"I have no idea what you're talking about."

"That Lance is getting married."

Ace glared. "Where is he?"

"He be around." The Lightest of them all said.

Arbella took a deep breath. "Well that's good for him. I'm glad he found happiness because–"

"We getting married too!" Ace interrupted.

Arbella looked at him in awe.

All of a few minutes ago and definitely over the past few weeks he made no attempt to take things to the next level. So hearing this now without an official proposal was disturbing.

"Is that right?" The Brownest of them all said, as she suppressed a laugh.

"Yep. And it's going to be the richest, most expensive wedding ever." Ace continued.

"Well Arbella is a lucky girl because your vocabulary and the way you made the announcement was poignant." The Lightest laughed before looking at her friend and back at him and his wild curly hair.

Ace's pressure rose. "Fuck is so funny?"

"We didn't mean to be offensive." The Brownest said. "Are you triggered or something?"

"Why do people do that? Say dumb shit and then get mad if somebody pops. Like what if I got up and slapped the shit out of you right now?"

"Ace!" Arbella yelled.

"Don't Ace me."

"Girl, I don't know what's going on, but I wasn't trying to upset your boyfriend."

"Lexi, just get your dumb ass away from my table."

Lexi, the Brownest of them all, sighed. "You know what, now I see why he left you for that white girl."

"What, bitch?" Ace said, rising from the table.

Arbella jumped up and grabbed his hand. Looking at the girls she said, "Just leave."

"We already gone." They turned to walk away but paused and looked back at him. "Nice suit by the way. We should hire you for my little sister's party. She loves clowns." They giggled deeper into the restaurant before disappearing out of sight.

When they reclaimed their seats he said, "Are you ready for us to get married? Because them hoes not about to rain on our shit."

She shook her head. "That was the tackiest wedding proposal I ever had in my life. In front of bitches I don't like or care about anymore. And if you think I'm going to say yes behind that shit then you don't know me at all."

She got up from the table, leaving him alone.

Ace drove down the street in his Benz truck looking for Arbella. He knew she couldn't have gone far, and so he couldn't wait to snap on her when he found her for leaving him alone. His rise and fall of emotions had him missing Walid more than ever, and so he made a call.

The phone rang twice.

"Why you calling so late?" Blakeslee whispered in her cell. "You said you would only call when you knew father would be gone."

"I had to hit you. To see what you up to."

"You didn't call for me. Once again you wanna talk to Walid, don't you?"

Out of the entire beef with his family, being isolated from his twin is what caused him so much pain.

"He still mad at me?" He said turning left on his continued hunt for Arbella.

"I don't know. He doesn't talk to me much about you and for the most part he spends all his time with Aliyah. But the real reason I think he can't speak to you is because father told us not to."

"He's really making me mad. Who separates brother from brother?"

"I 'on't know. Maybe you should talk to him. Tell him just because he cut you off doesn't mean that we should be cut off too. We miss you, Ace. I know I do."

"I don't know about that." He sighed.

"I think it's worth a try, Ace. I mean what do you got to lose?"

My pride. He thought.

After getting off the phone with her he bit the bullet and called Banks. The moment he answered and heard his deep voice he got scared. But he stayed the course. "I know you mad at me but–"

"Who is this?"

Ace's jaw twitched. Because he was positive he knew his son's voice. "It's me."

"What do you want?"

"I think it's unfair that you won't let me talk to my family."

"Unfair huh?"

"Yes. 'Cause even if you angry with me, why does everybody else have to be?"

"You mean besides the fact that you put everybody at risk by coming here? Resulting in Minnesota's husband not being alive. Nah, son, unfair is how you abandoned this family and thought only about yourself. Unfair is how selfish you have been for all your life. And unfair is how I'm only realizing it just now."

"It's not right you–"

By T. Styles

"Don't call me again. I'll reach out when I want to see how you're doing. And don't call a member of *my* family either."

"How you gonna reach out to me? You don't know where I am."

Banks laughed.

"One day you're going to regret doing what you're doing to me."

Banks chuckled again. "I guess we're going to see."

CHAPTER SEVEN
WALID

"I'm growing impatient."

Walid was standing in his room pacing, while waiting on his fiancé to enter. She had been out all night with Sydney and didn't bother hitting him to say if she was okay. When she finally walked inside he was enraged when he smelled the liquor oozing from her pores.

With bed hair and a wobbly walk, she leaned against the doorframe and said, "Hey, husband."

He was disgusted.

"The sitter had to take care of our son while I was helping father with some business ventures."

She plucked off one shoe and then the other before flopping on the bed. Drunk boots, she slipped to the floor and slithered back up. "So...so...shoe...I mean what's the problem?"

"This not like you." He stepped closer.

"How would you know what I'm like?" She slipped one arm out of her strappy dress and her titty popped out. "You never let me have no fun."

He moved closer. "Come again?"

"I mean really, Walid. I go out with a member of this family and it's a big deal? We should–"

"Joey is having problems with his wife. And the last thing I need is for that to reflect on us. For real, if she's going to do this kind of thing I don't want you around her. She's a bad influence."

"What did she do? Except invited me boat...I mean out?"

"And you don't know how to handle it."

"Luckily for me I'm grown and you can't tell me what to do."

"Either you're drunk or stupid right now. Whatever it is, I'm growing impatient."

"Walid, sit your ass down somewhere before I–."

He crashed his fist into the wall, halting her next words. The air between them grew as hard and as cold as an iceberg.

"People think you're always sweet, but they don't know you like I do, do they?" She said.

His breath quickened.

"Sometimes you scare me."

"I never laid a hand on you."

"For now. But you don't own me. You're not God."

"If you think I will be with a loose woman, then we can call it quits right now."

"So you...you breaking up with me?"

Silence.

She got up and stumbled toward him before falling in his arms. With warm vodka laced breath in his face she said, "Listen, I didn't mean to disrespect you or our relationship."

"What about Baltimore?"

"I didn't mean to disrespect our son either. But we were trapped on that island for so long that I wanted just a little taste of freedom. Don't you get it?"

"You never used the word trapped before."

"Well I'm doing it now."

"Listen, I get that you want to have fun. But coming home drunk is not something I'm willing to tolerate." He stroked her arms. "If you want to be with me this will never happen again."

"Don't be so—"

"Tell me you understand, Aliyah." His eyes zeroed on her with extreme intensity.

"I understand."

He nodded and walked out.

"You need to get back with your brother before we all suffer," she said quietly to herself before she threw up in her own mouth.

━━━━✈━━━━

It was a long night.

Mason and Banks were sitting in the lounge drinking whiskey. In between sips, Banks' eyes were glued on his phone per usual. He was unfocused and sloppy which wasn't his brand.

This was dangerous.

In fact, his behavior was so out of line that Mason was concerned that he was getting, well, *old.*

"What's your plan?" Mason sighed, taking a large sip.

Banks looked at him briefly but returned his eyes to his cell phone. "If you have a question, ask me directly."

"Okay." He placed his glass down. "What is your plan for our son?"

Banks sat his phone screen down. "He called."

"Okay, did you invite him home?"

"He was only concerned about Walid."

He nodded. "Well he shares his exact DNA so..."

"That's not good enough. He needs to see that we are the ones who provide the lifestyle he is accustomed to. I mean, where is he living now? How is he keeping his head afloat? Who's financing this shit?"

"Maybe the girl."

"Her father is a two-bit drug dealer and his daughter just lost all her businesses in that fire. So he has to be doing something else."

"What are your plans, Banks?"

"What do you want me to say?"

"I believe the question was straightforward enough. It's obvious you have a plan and I would like to know what it entails."

"I can't sit idly by and watch him destroy himself. I know I said I could but I...I can't." He looked down.

"He's an adult."

"Nineteen does not a man make."

Mason took a sip. He was trying his best to be easy with his words and at the same time he realized that the only language Banks respected was straightforward. "You are going to destroy your relationship with him beyond repair."

78 By T. Styles

"You don't even know what I'm doing."

"I know enough to know that whatever you got planned will go against what he wants. And if it goes against what he wants then that will be a problem in this family. Is that a risk you want to take?"

Banks stood up and took his and Mason's glass over to the bar. He filled them both up with thousand-dollar whiskey before handing Mason his and then taking his seat in front of the fireplace they hadn't lit.

Yet both could still see the flames.

"What I'm doing involves me making life difficult for him so that he will come back. I don't trust him out here alone, Mason. We haven't given him the skills necessary to deal with the world that has hatred for the rich, black, and beautiful. I need him to get his life together. I need him back home."

"Why?"

"Because...I never went into a lot of detail with you about my mother."

"When we were younger you did."

"Well, I think, I think he may be exhibiting signs of being bipolar. Why else would he flip so quickly?"

"So now he has mental illness because–."

"Father, when are we going back to the island?" Walid interrupted as he stormed into the lounge. He was filled with all the anxiety in the world.

Banks sat his glass down on the brass martini table. "What's going on?"

"I'm just ready to go home." He began pacing in front of both Mason and Banks. "I don't like nothing about it here."

Banks felt him on that shit.

"And I think things about to get bad," he added.

"Son, there is nothing more that I want than to return to our island. But we can't do that before your brother comes to his senses. So we have to–"

"So why don't we just go? Let Ace make his own bed and get into it no matter how nasty, dirty, and bloody it gets."

Mason didn't like his tune. "I realize you're upset but he's still your brother." He spoke. "You have to remember that when it's all said and done. Be careful, Walid."

"Is he though? Because if he was my brother he would know that doing what he's doing is destroying everything that both of you built. I don't like it here. I don't feel like this is home. And I want to leave."

"Did something happen between you and Aliyah?" Mason responded.

He looked down.

"Son, what happened?" Banks asked.

"She's hanging out with Joey's wife."

Banks and Mason looked at one another finally understanding his dismay.

"And this concerns you?" Banks questioned.

"Greatly, father. Joey hasn't been doing well with Sydney. And my concern is that she's going to take that out on mine."

"Son, if it's that easy for her to destroy your bond, is that someone you really want to keep on your arm?" Mason responded. "Because I know you both call each other husband and wife, but as of now you still aren't. And relationships, the ones that last must stand the test of time."

Banks nodded.

"She's all I know." He sounded desperate and as if he were running out of time.

"That's because you're young." Banks said. "But I assure you if she's not the right one you will find a better one in time. You're black. Rich. Handsome and powerful. But more than anything you have heart. That makes you a rare catch."

Walid wanted to go deeper. It felt good talking to them both. "I need help. What can I say to her to–."

Banks' phone rang. He stood and accepted it. "Speak."

Mason and Walid waited impatiently.

Banks smiled. Which was something no one had seen him do in a while. "Good. Now keep your eyes on him and don't let him out of your sight."

Mason sat back and dragged a hand down his face.

Silence.

"No, don't approach him either." Banks continued the call. "Don't say anything to him or even let him see you. I'll reach back out soon. In the meantime, tell your family goodbye, because until my son comes back, this is your life."

Banks ended the call.

"Is everything okay?" Mason asked.

"Follow me and I'll give you the details."

"Fathers, I need your help with my situation," Walid interrupted. "Please."

"Not right now, son. Just remember what I said. She might not be the one." He left out of the lounge, with Mason following quickly behind.

CHAPTER EIGHT
JOEY
"I miscalculated and realized I don't have it to spare."

Joey and Sydney were in their bedroom.

He had a large black suitcase on the bed and was packing quickly.

"Are you going to at least tell me what's going on?" She begged.

Every time she spoke the space filled with the odor of liquor. Which was becoming a common thing with her, as well as her weight gain.

"I already told you." He was disgusted. "If you weren't so drunk and fat you would have heard me in the first place. I mean why you been drinking so much anyway? It's like you want to kill yourself."

She looked down. "I just needed someone to talk to. And I wanted to hang out with my sister-in-law. Is it a problem?"

"I'm an addict, Sydney. You know that. Remember? We met in rehab. And being around this right now when we have a family crisis is too much. Still, what's going on at this minute is not about you. It's about my family."

"Joey, I just need you to pause for five seconds. Please."

He looked at her, took a deep breath and flopped on the edge of the bed. "I got ten minutes. That's it."

"For my sake it'll have to be enough."

"What do you want to talk about, Sydney?"

She sat next to him and wiped her blond hair from her face. "You're saying you are leaving so that you can help your family. Which will make me safe because you won't be around. But wouldn't I be safer with you?"

"No."

"I don't get it though."

"What do you want me to say? If I could go into more detail I would but things may pop off and I'm leaving here so you'll be fine."

"I remember the stories of the Wales family beefs you spoke about. Which led to your addiction. But as far as I see now, the only problem is Ace."

"And?"

"Well based on your theory to leave me here alone, if I'm in danger, all the wives should be in danger too. And the children. Instead they are all where you're going. To Banks' new estate."

84   By T. Styles

He got up and started packing again.

"You couldn't even give me the full ten minutes?"

"I miscalculated and realized I don't have it to spare."

"Suddenly I don't feel guilty anymore."

When his phone rang he stopped and answered.

It was Banks.

"I'm on the way, pops."

"On the way where?"

He looked at her and then walked toward the corner of the room. "After we spoke, I figured it would be easier for me to help if I was living with you."

"So is Sydney coming too?"

"No. We thought it was best for her to stay."

Sydney may not have heard the entire conversation, but she heard that lie.

"Do you know anybody who can do what we talked about earlier? I want to escalate things with Ace."

"I thought you weren't going that route anymore."

"After I spoke to Mason, and found his new location, I changed my mind. Plus Walid is getting anxious. So, I think the girl is the anchor. I want to attack."

"Yeah I have a couple options."

"Well put it in play."

"No problem."

"And Joey."

"Yes, pops."

"I don't know what's going on over there but don't forget she's your wife. That means you made her a Wales. I don't want to see you make the same mistakes I did with your mother by leaving her when she needed me the most. And I don't want her anger spilling onto the other women in our family."

He looked at Sydney who was wiping her tears away. "Understood, pops. But she's harmless. Trust me."

When he ended the call he grabbed his suitcase and walked toward the door. Before leaving she said, "You're going back to the island when this is all said and done aren't you? And you're going without me."

"You never wanted to go remember?"

Silence.

He took a deep breath and said, "I'll let you know when I get there."

86   By T. Styles

He walked out.

Frustrated and in emotional pain she picked up her phone. It rang a few times before Aliyah finally answered. "What are you doing right now?"

"Nothing. Baltimore is asleep and I'm still trying to come down from the hangover. Why? You sound sad."

"You feel like drinking some coffee with me?"

"Sure. Come on over and I'll make us a pot. Besides, I'd love to have you."

Sydney and Aliyah were drinking Kopi Luwak in the dining room, which cost $600 a pound. Made from coffee cherries that have been eaten, digested, and pooped out by the Asian palm civet, an animal that looked like a cross between a cat and a raccoon, it was a delicacy.

The two loved the taste and indulged in it often.

"So what happened?" Aliyah asked, as she poured more cream and sugar into her cup.

"Joey has been isolating me." She sipped her entire drink and poured another. "And I'm afraid if he divorces me, I'll lose this family. And I'll lose you too."

Just then they could hear Joey and his brothers talking and laughing in the background.

"Does he know you're here?" Aliyah whispered.

"No."

"Thank God for mansions."

They laughed quietly.

"Listen, no matter what goes on between you and Joey you will always have me as family. Us wives have to stick together."

"Even if he divorces me?"

"Yep, because then you'll just be my friend." She placed a warm hand over hers. "And I love my friends more."

They hugged one another and Sydney cried in her arms.

By T. Styles

CHAPTER NINE
WALID
"I hate that name."

Walid was playing against Patrick in a video game. He was whipping him up so badly it wasn't even funny. And as a result, just like his father who he only met as a baby, Patrick got angry.

"All you do is cheat." Patrick pouted.

"Lil nigga, shut up. If you can't handle it, say that but don't act like I'm cheating out here."

"But you are though. That's the only way you can beat me."

Walid laughed it off. Besides he and Patrick would go on for days sometimes playing games. And each time he would complain upon losing that Walid was cheating.

"If this family broke up, I'd choose Ace." He said in anger to throw him off his chi.

Walid frowned. "What you talking about?"

"Well me and The Triad been thinking..."

"I hate that name."

"It's just a way for y'all to know who I'm talking about." He paused. "Anyway, we been thinking that Ace freer being out there then we are in here. And I want to see what that feels like."

Walid positioned his body to look at him. Dropping the controller he said, "Listen, Ace can front all he wants but he's having a hard time out there. 'Cause ain't nothing more important than family. Nothing."

When Walid's phone rang and he saw an unknown number he realized who it was.

"Wait, you get to have a cell phone too?" Patrick asked.

"I'm nineteen so it's different." He paused. "Now get some practice so I can whoop up on you again."

"Tell Ace I said hi."

Walid glared. If there was even talk that he was speaking to Ace it could mean other parts of his family would break down. Bad enough he was having issues with his wife. He definitely didn't need to have issues with his father too.

"And the next time you lie on me, I'ma crack your jaw." Walid threatened.

Fear took over Patrick's body.

When Walid was sure he had his heart, he walked out.

Going to the bathroom where he knew he wouldn't be bothered, he answered. "Why you gotta keep calling me?" He whispered.

"You mean why I keep calling my twin? The one person on Earth who I shared the same womb with? You sound crazy."

"I'm still waiting on an answer."

"I'm getting married."

"I'm trying to figure out why you telling me."

"Because I need you to be my best man."

"Let me make it clear, twin. There will never come a time where I'll stand at your side ever again."

"This is dumb! Why are you mad with me?"

"Because of you we here. Because of you, there's problems. If you want to make shit right, come back home."

"Nah. Won't be doing that."

"Why not though? You can't possibly tell me you're happy. If you were you wouldn't be bothering me."

What he didn't know was at the moment he was still searching for his girl who left the restaurant after his half ass proposal. Still, in his mind at least he had freedom. Even if his idea of freedom wasn't picture perfect.

"Nigga, what do you want?" Walid said a bit louder.

"You know what I find odd?"

Walid took a deep breath.

"I forgave you for what you did to me." Ace paused. "By taking my girl. Yet you would let this come between us."

"She was mine the moment she looked into my eyes."

Silence.

"And people are dead, Ace. Minnesota doesn't have a husband and she hasn't been out of the room since."

"From what I heard about her past she'll be all right. Let Spacey keep her warm at night."

He frowned. "You talking ill of your sister?"

"I'm just saying she'll get another dude or brother lover. Maybe you can lay the dick since you enjoy coming to the rescue."

"If you ever–."

"But if we talking about the dead, what about the old man you ran over with your truck?" Ace continued.

Walid was dizzy with rage.

"You shouldn't be talking about that, Ace. Father warned us all."

92

"He doesn't know the entire story either does he?" Ace chuckled. "It's not like I'm the only one that committed murder. Well, murder in the sense anyway." He paused. "In my situation, Zercy walked in of his own free will to save me. He got shot and killed for his weak ass efforts. But when that old man died, it was because you ran him over."

"Where you want me to meet you again?"

"Tomorrow, I'll text you the address."

Walid nodded sinisterly. "I can't wait."

CHAPTER TEN
BANKS
"It'll just take a little bit more time."

Banks and Spacey sat in the boardroom with Kordell going over the plans to turn his drug money legit.

Prior to doing business, Banks believed Kordell possessed intelligence to evade being locked up while still running a drug business for so long. But now he realized luck alone must have been on the man's side.

Banks was annoyed how every time Kordell opened his mouth, the word *titties* or *pussy* dropped out. It was difficult to process what he wanted with his valuable time. Because if it was just strip clubs, Banks felt he could have at it alone.

"Trust me, Banks, this will work. I finally got an idea that will suit both of us."

"Nothing has to be suitable for me. I'm wealthy already."

"Exactly." Spacey responded.

"Okay I'm just saying I finally get what you mean by needing an app. But what about, instead

By T. Styles

of the things on this list, the app gave men something to look at no matter where they were. Like, it's for adult entertainment. What's the harm in that?"

"Porn?" Spacey said.

"Let me put it like this. There is no way in this lifetime I will help you or anybody else build an app like that. And even if I did, I'm one hundred percent sure it won't work."

Kordell flopped back. "You wrong, Banks."

"I'm not. As a matter of fact I'm over it at this point. So let me be clear, and I'ma need you to listen because I won't say it again."

Kordell nodded.

"Unless you get with the program...my program...I'm done."

"I never took you for a man who didn't compromise. That's gonna be a problem for you in the future."

"Do you understand what I'm saying? 'Cause I'm not going back and forth after tonight. I don't have the time."

Kordell nodded, looked at his men and focused back on Banks. "Okay so what do we do now?"

"The person who runs the app company we need is extremely busy. But she's vital because anything that she puts her attention on will be automatically considered legit. So the likelihood of the authorities, or anybody downplaying your business, will be slim."

"So let's get her."

"Right now she's not available."

Kordell sighed. "So why did you bring her up if we can't get her?"

"Never said I couldn't get her. It'll just take a little bit more time. So until then–"

Suddenly Joey rushed into the meeting and Banks rose.

"Getting kind of irritated at how every time we are in our meeting a member of the Wales family interrupts. I deserve a little more than that."

Banks ignored him altogether and focused on his son.

"I found the perfect person." Joey said. He pulled out his phone and Banks looked at who was on the screen.

He smiled. "I think this will do."

"So are you sure you want me to go through with the plan? I was speaking to Mason earlier and he's against what we talked about."

"Tell me something I don't know already."

In the background Kordell breathed heavily like a puppy doing all he could to gain attention. Paws slapping about the boardroom table.

Again, he was ignored.

"You know I'm going to do whatever you tell me to do, pops. But I have to be honest, something about the press we're about to put on him makes me think it may backfire."

"Ace is my son. He's not smarter or richer than me."

"Aren't you the one who told me never to underestimate your opponent?"

"That's just it, he's not my opponent. He's not even in the ring. So just do what I ask and let me know what happens."

Joey nodded and walked out.

Kordell barked.

CHAPTER ELEVEN
WALID
"I don't know what you want me to say."

Walid was heated.

He was tired of how Ace thought it was sweet to blackmail him over something that happened in the past.

Especially when it was Ace's fault the old man died.

Years ago, Ace got himself into trouble off Wales Island. As usual Walid came to the rescue. After being chased by an angry mob to get Ace away from the scene, Walid accidentally struck the man. It wasn't until later that they discovered that that man injured, who later died, was Aliyah's father. And Walid was certain that if she ever found out she would dump him for good.

So the fact that Ace hung this over his head troubled him dearly.

His plan was simple.

The moment he saw Ace, he would steal him in his jaw to let him know that the blackmailing shit would end there. Sure he was certain that they would scrap. But he also knew that when they sparred in boxing rings in the past, that he was always the victor and Ace was always flat on his back.

Walid parked haphazardly and jumped out of his car. He was outside of a shopping district with a lot of eateries and clothing boutiques, but he figured it was as good a place as any.

And then he spotted him.

Ace smiled but it didn't take him long to realize that with the frown on Walid's face, this was not a pleasant meeting.

Fists clenched; Walid was almost upon him when Arbella stepped out of the restaurant. "What are you doing out here?" She asked Ace.

It was obvious she was still angry from the night of the terrible wedding proposal because a huge frown was on her face too.

Walid and Arbella both paused when they saw one another.

After all, she had sex with Walid under the guise that he was Ace. It was a dirty trick played on her although at the time, the Wales family felt it necessary since she alone had information they needed to find Ace.

They hadn't seen each other since he came inside of her body.

And for now the punishment Walid planned would have to wait.

"Hello, brother." Ace said. "I want you to officially meet my girl." He dropped his arm around her neck.

Walid didn't know whether to smile or to frown. The entire meeting threw him off and at the same time he felt bad for what he'd done to her. At the end of the day she was an innocent bystander in a fight that he was certain would get more out of control each day.

Walid extended his hand as if they'd never officially met. "Nice to meet you."

She shook it quickly and looked down immediately.

Walid wondered why.

"Listen, can we talk in private?" Walid asked Ace.

Ace placed a heavy hand on his shoulder and said, "Sure. But first let's get some drinks and some food up in us." He rubbed his belly. "I need you to help stop my girl from being mad at me."

"Ace, please stop," she said.

"I don't have time for--."

"Walid, I want you to get to know your sister-in-law." Ace smiled brighter. It was like he was in a romance movie, while they were in a thriller.

Had she not been there, Walid would have ripped into him but again there was the awkward atmosphere regarding her and him making love.

"Brother, I want to know right now, is this beef between us forever?" Ace pressed.

Silence.

"Walid, are you intent on hating me for the rest of your life?"

Walid looked at Arbella and Ace and decided to avoid the question. Instead he said, "I only got a few minutes."

"Sold!" Ace said, as if he was bidding on his time.

Five minutes later Walid and Arbella were sitting directly across from one another with Ace sitting next to her.

"You have to admit, I nailed it when I picked her right?" Ace bragged. "I mean look at her fine ass."

Walid looked at her and quickly at him. "I don't know what you want me to say."

"To be honest there is nothing to say. Outside of you're absolutely right."

"She's beautiful. Is that what you wanted to hear?"

"Easy, brother." He said, putting his hands up, playfully. "This one is taken."

Walid was growing so annoyed his skin reddened. "At this point I'm getting tired of your shit, Ace. You said you wanted to talk and–"

Ace stood up and got on one knee on the side of Arbella. Whipping a fat ass diamond ring out of his pocket he said, "Arbella Valentine, in front of my twin brother, I offer you my heart."

Nah, I'm good. She thought.

"What you doing, nigga," Walid said. "Ain't nobody come here for all this."

"Shhhhh." He smiled, wild hair flopping, per usual. Focusing back on her he said, "Would you do me the honor of being my wife?"

She nodded just to get him up.

Ace was embarrassed. "You gotta say the words though."

"Yes."

He slid the ring on her finger and flopped back in his seat. "Welp, it's official."

"Are you crazy?" Walid asked.

"Arbella? Is that you?" A man about 6 '3 said walking up to the table.

"Who are you?" She questioned.

He walked over to her side and frowned. "So we really going to play them games? Where you pretend you don't know me? Okay let's do it like this..." He planted a kiss on her lips and Ace knocked over the table trying to get at him.

"Fuck is wrong with you!" He shoved him off.

Even Walid who was at odds with his brother stood ready to attack.

"I'm sorry, but who are you again?" The stranger asked.

Arbella was so afraid of what was happening she trembled.

"It doesn't matter who I am. Bounce before there'll be a problem."

He didn't bounce.

Instead he continued to make his play on Arbella.

Wrong move.

Ace hit him in his face and followed it up with a blow to his stomach. When he positioned his body to fight back, Walid got in the middle and struck him in the center of the nose.

He advanced no more.

It was a technique they learned in Belize, which temporarily blinded the person immediately.

He regained a few of his bearings but Walid looked him square in the eyes. "If I were you, I would leave while I still can."

The Stranger glared, looked down at Arbella and stormed off. Blood splattering along the way.

Mostly embarrassed at the possibility of his new fiancé looking like a whore in front of his twin he yelled at her. "Who the fuck was that?"

Still sitting down she said, "I...I don't know what's going on. I don't know who that is. I'm so confused."

"Just like you didn't know them bitches who came over and mentioned your ex-boyfriend marrying some whore?"

"Ace, all I want to do is take care of you. I'm concerned that–"

He smacked her silent.

Shocked, Walid shoved him clear across the restaurant. He fell on a newlywed couple's table, and mashed potatoes and gravy smeared the back of his jeans and shirt.

Ace immediately got up as the two brothers squared off.

Face to face.

"You really want to lose a fight in front of your pretty fiancé?" Walid questioned.

Ace breathed heavily, looked down at her and back at him. "You can't have this one. This time, she really belongs to me."

Walid glared. "You do what you want when you're not around me. But I'm not about to let you beat on a female for no reason in my presence."

"Oh, I need a reason?"

"You know what I mean."

"Like I said you can't have this one. And the next time you put your hands on me in that way there might be gunplay."

"Hold up, are you threatening me?" He asked through clenched teeth. "You saying the next time I see you blood gotta spill?"

"You heard what I said right?"

"Loud and clear."

Walid walked toward the door and doubled back. "Oh, and speaking of gun play, that's the last time you gonna threaten me about what happened on the island with the old man. Because as far as the family knows, you killed the stranger. Not me."

"We both know the truth though, don't we?"

"Why busy myself with the truth when a lie will do." Looking down at Arbella, Walid said, "It only gets worse from here. If I were you, I'd leave him while I still can."

He stormed away.

ACE

Arbella came running into their penthouse with Ace hot on her heels. The moment the door closed, he grabbed her by both arms and shook her as if he was trying to release dimes from a piggy bank.

Through clenched teeth and wild ass hair he asked. "Who the fuck was that nigga?"

"I...I already told you I don't know!" She cried, the engagement ring sparkling.

"It sure didn't seem like that to me!"

"You hit me!"

"Because you provoked me."

She walked away and flopped on the sofa. She couldn't believe this was her life. "My mother once cared for a jealous man. She paid for it with a burned face. I won't make the same mistake she did."

"You belong to me. So we've gone past that already."

By T. Styles

"No, we haven't. Is this why you want me away from my father? So you can hurt me?"

"You mean the same jealous man you were just speaking about? That you love so much more than me?"

"At least he's getting help. He told me himself."

His eyes widened. "So you've been seeing him?"

"No...I told you I wouldn't."

"Good, because I don't trust you around him."

"Why, Ace?" Huge tears poured down her cheeks. "Why are you so intimidated by powerful men? Is it jealousy? I mean, you haven't even said you were sorry for hitting me!"

"You need to know something about me up front. Because I don't want to talk about this ever again. If I do something, chances are I meant to do it. So even if you get a fake apology out of me it won't be sincere. The question is do you prefer the truth or a lie?"

"If you ever hit me again we are over."

"You not going nowhere. And who was the nigga who kissed you?"

"I don't know! I said it a million times. The only person I was with before you was Lance. If there was someone else in the past I would have told you. I'm not out to hurt you. I'm out to protect you. To love you. But you're making it hard."

"How come I don't believe you?"

She took a deep breath. "My mother once told me that the hardest thing to do was to love a person who doesn't love themself. That the work required to get through to that kind of person drains the soul."

"I don't want to hear all that shit."

"You're going to hear it anyway. Don't make me fall out of love for you. I'm moving dangerously close."

He looked down. "If I find out that you were with my brother–"

Her heart thumped.

"Has it ever occurred to you that whoever the person was that interrupted our dinner was sent by your father? And that it has nothing to do with me? Think about it. I'm not the enemy, Ace."

He blinked a few times.

It was the first thing she said that got through and he flopped next to her. Looking over at her he said, "You really gonna leave me?"

She sighed.

"You know you can't do that girl." He touched her leg.

108   By T. Styles

She shoved his hand off. "Stop, Ace."

"You can't leave me," he said softly.

"I'm moving toward it."

He got up, pushed the sliding door open and walked out on their balcony. The city yelled at him to take his ass back in from below.

"Then if you do I'll jump." He straddled the railing.

Her heart rocked. "Ace, stop playing." She rushed out, begging him with her entire being to cease the madness.

"If you don't want me, what is there to live for?" And since they were thirteen floors high if he jumped it would be over. "Tell me you love me, girl or I'll jump."

"I love you!" Her white palms faced him as more tears poured down her cheeks. "It will kill me if you die! Pleassssssse!"

"I don't believe you."

"It's true! Please don't do this!" She dropped to her knees, the concrete ground rubbing roughly at her flesh. "Please get down!"

He slowly got off, helped her to her feet and pulled her toward him. He could see in her eyes she meant every word. His dick hardened at what was revealed.

"You gonna die if I die?" His ego was on full display.

"Yes. But you can't keep..."

He kissed her silent.

It was so passionate, that he pushed her back against the wall to the left of the balcony. The rush of the city and the wind played in the background like music. Wanting more, he laid down.

"Is that pussy wet?" He tugged at her hand, pulling her down towards the concrete.

She straddled him, looking down at his handsome yet crazy face. "Ace, you are..."

"I asked are you wet?" He slithered his finger under her dress and into her panties. "Yeah, you wet."

A huge tear fell on his lip, and he licked it away. "Ace, I don't know if I can keep–."

"I love you." He whispered. "And you can't leave me. Not now. Not ever."

Tears continued to fall from her eyes and dampened his cheeks.

"I do love you." She lowered her body and kissed his lips. Her long hair brushed the sides of his face. He removed her panties before pulling his stiff and pulsating dick from his boxers.

Her legs widened to allow him access.

110   **By T. Styles**

He gained entry.

"Ace, you have to get…"

He went deep, and her mouth widened. It felt sooo good. "Mmmmmm."

Fear, mixed with being out on the balcony and the love she had in her heart for him caused her to question her own sanity.

In and out he pushed as he felt his body revving up. Although she was scared, she was still juicy as if the whole thing had been foreplay.

Had it?

It's amazing how fear can rev up the body's mechanics, confusing the mind and heart. In this case despite wanting nothing but peace in life her soul had been awakened by a madman.

Why did he feel so good? She thought as he continued to pump in and out of her, with hands on her hips.

She knew she needed to get away from this man as far as possible and at the same time she was certain that if she left he would officially be alone.

And that she could never find a love greater or more passionate.

They continued their fuck session until he placed a hand on her lower back and pressed downward. This positioned her clit on top of his dick as he glided back and forth, causing her to tingle in a way she had never done before.

There was no doubt that he knew her sexually, inside, and out. Since they'd been together she suffered multiple orgasms because of him.

But this was by far the hardest and most passionate experience she ever had in her life.

But in the midst of it all, a question lingered.

If they stayed together, would he kill her?

Or would she have to kill him to be free?

By T. Styles

CHAPTER TWELVE
BANKS
"He's a part of a set."

B anks was sitting in his office when Mason walked inside...

"You're still working? We normally have a glass by now." When he looked toward the right of his desk he saw he already started. "Looks like you forgot to invite me."

"Never."

"What's going on?"

There was a look of satisfaction on Banks' face as he busied himself with documents. "I got caught up on Kordell's project."

"And why are you happy again?"

"She's coming over tonight. For Kordell."

Mason walked in and sat in the chair across from his desk. "Who you talking about? Because when it comes to Kordell I gotta admit, I don't give a fuck."

"The app designer. After getting my employees involved with trying to solicit her business it turns out all I had to do was call personally and suddenly she was available."

"Again, why you happy?"

"Because once she designs this app we can go back home. And after Ace comes to his senses, we'll officially be free."

"Even if he doesn't fly with us?"

He looked up from his paperwork. "He's going to come. I need my son back with me. He's part of a set."

"You losing touch with reality. I heard from Joey you sent a nigga to kiss Ace's bitch."

He chuckled once. "And?"

"What are you? Fifteen?"

"Father, can I go out?" Blakeslee asked, entering the office. "If my handler oversees to make sure I don't abuse privileges?"

Banks sighed. "Why are you so obsessed with going outside?" He fiddled with more documents.

"I wouldn't call it obsessed."

"You sure about that? Because I do."

"Father, not everything is about our small little world. Some things are bigger and—"

"The answer is no. And if I find out you've been out, I'm going to hurt you."

"That's not fair!"

"Fair or not, I've protected you from the harshest forms of punishment because you are a

114 By T. Styles

girl. I tell you to not antagonize our employees, you do it anyway. I told you not to go out the front door, I caught you on the camera twerking. I'm growing tired of your disrespect. So if you break one of my rules again, you are gonna see a side of me you never have."

Silence.

"Don't leave this house or else."

"I hate it here!" She yelled running off.

Mason shook his head and smiled. "Every time I look at her I'm pulled into the past."

"What you mean?" Banks continued looking at more documents.

"What I mean? She looks exactly like you back in the day. Same face. Same name. Everything."

Banks paused for a minute. "You know what? I can't remember how I looked. I can barely remember being in high school."

He didn't believe him. "Are you serious?"

Banks nodded. "The only thing I remember from the past is you."

He took a deep breath. "Do you think it's a brain thing again?"

"I don't know." Banks sighed. "And the worst part about it is I don't care."

When the doorbell rang and Banks glanced down at his security cameras, he hit a button for the intercom. A Benz came into view. "Let her in and then take her to the lounge. I'll be there in a second."

"You're taking her to the lounge?"

"Yep! Because after she designs Kordell's app I have some ideas for apps for myself too. This is a big deal."

"I wish I could be excited as you are."

Banks winked. "I'm excited enough for the both of us. We going home, friend! I feel it!"

Five minutes later, they were in the lounge with Faye Armstrong. Wearing a black one-piece business dress with a red suit jacket which did nothing to hide her curves, Banks was stunned by her attractiveness.

Her brown skin was almost absent of makeup, and her real black hair hung straight down her back like a recently paved road.

He couldn't get enough of her quiet beauty.

Getting down to business, she and Banks sat on the sofa in the lounge, overlooking the ideas for Kordell's app, while Mason noticed something brewing between them.

"...these aren't the only ideas I have, Mr. Wales," she blushed, before taking a strand of her hair and tucking it behind her ear. He was so damn fine she couldn't focus. "Just a few I think will help your client. I'm able to go deeper but this is the first time someone asked my personal opinion on ideas I think would lead to a successful app."

"Well from what you're showing me, my client will definitely be pleased. It's more important that we create an app that is scalable over a longer period of time. And the idea of producing NFT's with a few clicks of a finger may be helpful, but your idea provides a balance he will appreciate."

She nodded. "Coming from you, that's mind blowing."

Mason rolled his eyes.

Taking a deep breath she said, "Now there will be a lot of paperwork and approvals must go through. But with my business connections I'm sure it shouldn't be a problem."

Banks stared a bit longer at her before saying, "I trust you."

"How did you get started?" Mason spoke eager to get into a conversation which he was clearly excluded from.

Banks looked at him in disbelief. "Thought you weren't interested in Kordell's app?"

"I guess Faye is inspiring all of us."

She cleared her throat. "I taught myself how to design apps before I knew it'd be a big thing. Since then, I just continued to learn the business and before long a few popular Fortune 500 companies hired me. The apps were successful, making all of my clients overnight sensations and millionaires, and the rest was history."

Banks said, "It's refreshing that a woman as beautiful as you is so tech savvy."

"This nigga here." Mason said under his breath.

"These ideas are brilliant," Banks continued. "Mr. Wales–"

"Banks." He corrected her.

"Banks, you really are kind but I'm still learning the business. Which is why when I got your phone call I almost didn't accept."

"Why not?" He frowned.

"I feared I wouldn't live up to the hype."

He looked her over and with a wider smile said, "You most certainly did."

"Oh, God!" Mason said out loud. "Get a room already."

By T. Styles

Banks shot his head in his direction. "Something wrong?"

"You mean besides you and the tired ass lines you throwing at this young lady?"

"Father, we have to talk!" Walid said, rushing into the lounge.

Banks stood up, tapped his shoulder, before leading him outside of the lounge. He closed the door. Looking down on him he said, "What's up?"

"I want to say something to you." He shuffled a little. "Before I begin, I'm not trying to threaten you in any kind of way."

Banks' mood tightened.

"But if I talk to you as a man, and it's shot down, in the future things may never be the same."

"Fair enough." Banks nodded. "I'm listening."

"I saw Ace today."

He glared. "But I told everyone he was off limits. He chose to be outside of this family and so he needs to see what that *feels* like."

"I know but I had to because, well, there's something else." He took a deep breath. "Do you remember the man that Ace ran over years ago? Off the island. Who ended up dying?"

Banks looked behind him at the closed door and back at his son. "Do you also remember me saying never to bring it up again?"

"I do."

"So what are you doing?" He asked through clenched teeth.

"The accident was actually caused by me. And since you forbade us from talking about it I never got to tell you that the man that was killed was Aliyah's father."

"Aliyah's father?"

"Yes. And Ace is blackmailing me now because of the ban you have against us speaking to him."

Banks was livid. "He's always up to something. I still hold onto hope that he can change, but at this point I'm not sure." He walked a few steps away and returned. Dragging his hand down his face and dropping it at his side he said, "I don't know what makes him so evil. But I will protect you and this secret at all costs."

"Thank you, father. I just wanted to come to you. In case he tries to get me locked up or something. He's dangerous."

Banks didn't hear a word he said. In his mind Ace was still a child and could be handled as such.

By T. Styles

Banks took a deep breath. "I appreciate your honesty but during these times I need you to respect my rules. And what I'm ruling is that until he comes to his senses that you never talk to him again."

"You don't have to worry."

"Good." He nodded. "I'll come up with a plan for the man who died when the time is right." He looked at the door and back at him. "We're almost done here. I helped a client and when I bring Ace to his knees, we should be home for the long run."

Walid sighed in relief. "Before I forget, tonight there was someone who approached us while we were at the table. Some guy who claimed he knew Arbella. Ace's girl."

"And?"

"Was that your work, father?"

"Yes."

"Ace hit his girl. After the person you hired kissed her. Arbella may be with him but she's a nice person."

"I don't doubt that she is. But there are always casualties in every war. And the only thing I'm thinking about is getting Ace back to the island. She's the least of my concerns. For me, it's family over everything. I hope you understand."

He nodded although he was shocked at the levels Banks reached. He finally realized he had little knowledge about the man whose blood coursed through his own veins. "I understand."

Banks turned to walk back inside and then said, "Oh, and do me a favor before you settle in."

"Anything."

"Go check on your sister. She was angry with me earlier and we need to keep an eye open with her."

Walid sighed. "Anything but that."

He smiled. "Go, son."

BLAKESLEE

Blakeslee was in her closet Facetiming a boy named Eric.

At first she thought he was fake until he sent a picture of his face followed by a picture of his dick to let her know it was real. After some time, she realized that she liked speaking to him even though he spoke of sex more than she wanted if she would be honest.

By T. Styles

After all, Blakeslee was still a virgin.

But her need to be seen brought her dangerously close to exposing herself in sexual ways.

Not to mention, she preferred older boys.

"When are you going to show me what you said you were?" Eric spoke. He was dark skinned with low-cut hair and an earring so big it sparkled.

"I told you I will."

"Yeah but you said after we had 50 calls so you can make sure you trust me."

"Well, has it been 50 calls yet?"

"No, but I told you I don't like girls that are immature. If we gonna be together then you gotta act like grown folks do."

Blakeslee sighed. "This is me. You're not going to change me. I do what I want when I want, and I also told you that."

He was annoyed. "Girls like you always feel they can talk to dudes any kind of way."

"How is it any kind of way?"

"When pretty girls talk shit, guys feel like they can't say nothing back."

"Well that's stupid. If you gotta say something open your mouth."

"It might be stupid but it's true. I bet if you were not as attractive you wouldn't be giving me the blues the way that you are."

"You know, sometimes you talk old. I mean who says blues?"

He laughed. "That's just because I hang around my granddad a lot."

Her eyes lowered. "You know your grandfather?"

"Yeah, doesn't everybody?"

Blakeslee used the moment to think about the past.

Within seconds it became painfully obvious that she didn't know anybody outside of the people in the walls of the mansion. Her desire to know anything no matter how small, was what was causing her dangerous curiosity.

Banks hated the past and so he denied his children the past too.

Big mistake.

"Show me something right now and I'll show you something." She spoke in an effort to get her mind off 'feeling' pain.

"Are you going to play games like you did last time?"

"Nope. If you show me your dick I'll–"

By T. Styles

Suddenly the closet door came flying open.

Walid was standing above her with a look of hate on his face. Snatching the phone from her grasp he only caught a brief view of the boy before the teen hung up.

"You out here talking to niggas on the phone and shit?" He asked, showing her the blank screen.

"Why did you do that!" She stood up but fell toward the hanging clothing. They swallowed her up before her head peeped through again.

"I asked you a question!"

"I never get to do anything around here. Patrick, Bolt, and Riot are always too busy to spend time with me."

"What that got to do with you talking to a guy on the phone? Why do y'all come out here and lose your mind?"

"Y'all?"

"You and Aliyah!"

"Because I'm lonely!" She sniffled, standing up straight. "Is that so hard to understand?"

Walid stopped listening to her moments earlier. Instead, he was scanning through her phone and what he saw caused him to lose reason. She had different angles above her breasts. And he even spotted a picture which almost exposed her vagina.

None of them were *giving* but still...

When he raised his hand to show her the picture, the phone knocked against her face.

He didn't care.

"You sending nudes too?"

"You shouldn't have hit me." She said with a lowered brow. "And I'm going to tell father."

It was an accident, but he offered no apologies.

"Please do. Because that will give me all the reason in the world to show him these tired ass titty shots." He positioned the camera directly into her eyesight.

She turned away, not being able to look at her own nakedness.

"Give me my phone." She said through clenched teeth.

"Shut up, slut." He walked out and slammed the door, leaving her alone.

The moment he walked out and a few feet down the hallway, he felt guilt. Blakeslee was out of control but he knew it was a cry for help.

He turned back to talk to her but bumped into Minnesota instead. She was wearing a red robe with a red bonnet to match and her eyes were as dark as ever.

She also lost so much weight that she was almost unrecognizable.

"Sorry, sis. You good?"

"I'm fine. But are *you* okay?" She scanned him.

He was surprised to see her. "Oh, yeah...I'm...I'm fine too."

"You and I both know that's not true."

"For real, sis. I'm okay."

For a brief moment, he thought about telling her about Blakeslee. But he was tired of being at odds with his siblings. Because no matter how whorish Blakeslee was, and she was putting on like a slut, she was still his little sister. And so he would have to find a new way to deal with her.

"Okay, I won't press you." She said.

He was about to walk off but asked, "But how are you?"

"You mean since my husband was killed?"

"I really am sorry about that, Minnesota."

"I know, but it's not your fault. Ace was the one who brought us out here, not you."

He took a deep breath.

"And the flowers you've been sending me every few days are beautiful." She continued.

"I just wanted to give you a reason to smile. I would have knocked on your door but sometimes I feel like the best thing you can do is leave people alone while they are going through."

"That was the best thing about your gift. You understand me." She took a deep breath, hugged him, and walked away crying.

That interaction, although separate from Blakeslee, reminded him how precious sisters were.

And so for now he was going to let Blakeslee breathe even though he was angry he couldn't get her partially nude shots out of his mind.

By T. Styles

CHAPTER THIRTEEN
ACE
"You still wanna marry me?"

A ce and Arbella were at a wedding planner's office going over details for their celebration.

At first Ace was against the event, but he figured after some time that maybe getting married would show his brother that although he came to the states on some sneak shit, that at least he was making a real life for himself and his future wife.

He figured that with time, Walid would be unable to deny him and their bond would repair itself.

"Let me go get the rest of the palettes," the wedding planner said, excusing himself for a minute.

The brief silence between the fiancé's was awkward. Arbella seemed disconnected ever since they had sex on the balcony. Throw the whole wedding away was now her motto.

To calm her nerves, he agreed to see someone in the mental health field for his struggles although he had yet to follow through. "You still wanna marry me?" He asked. "'Cause you feel different."

She looked down and nodded.

"Arbella..."

"Yes, Ace. I do." She sighed deeply. "You really don't have to be here you know?" He stuck with her so hard lately, that she felt like she couldn't breathe.

"I know. But if we going to do this, we should do it together."

"So, I was thinking that maybe I should ask my father to walk me down the aisle."

He glared.

There she went with her daddy issues bullshit.

"You gonna bring up that nigga again when I told you it's dead? I'm the only man you need in your life. Have you been talking to him?"

"I promise to God I haven't."

He didn't believe her.

"Ace, it's the truth." She paused. "It's just that the last time I saw him he needed a little help to get by. And I want it back."

"Little help?" He thought for a minute. "Hold up, you gave him the money from the insurance when your shops blew up?"

By T. Styles

"Ace, I don't want to talk about finances with you."

"You sound stupid. Did you give him your money?"

"He said he would pay me back after–"

"Don't you see what this dude is doing?"

"It isn't what you think."

"It's exactly what I think. He only comes around when he thinks he can get something from you. This nigga really sold you to Lance. And if you weren't already mine, he would sell you to me too." He paused. "I'm not feeling the shit. And one day he's going to break your heart so much you won't be able to recover." His phone rang and he saw it was Blakeslee.

"Who is it?"

His nostrils flared. "My little sister."

"Take it. You kinda been ignoring her lately."

"You want to get me out of your face?"

"Ace."

He nodded and stepped to the side across from the open window. He could still see her though. "What's up, Blakeslee? I'm kinda busy right now."

She was crying so loudly you could hardly make out what she was saying. "He...choked me...hit me...and bit my arm."

She really put a spin on the truth.

"Calm down and tell me what happened slower."

"Walid...he...he...snapped. He choked me, bit me, and hit my arm."

This wasn't making sense. He knew Walid had a dark side. He'd seen it himself. But this account of events had him sounding like a wolf.

"Are you saying he laid hands on you?"

"Yes."

His temples throbbed. "Fuck for?"

"Because he found out I have a boyfriend and he was jealous."

She definitely left some details and added some shit that never occurred. But she was certain that if Ace knew about Eric's dick pic, that he wouldn't be much happier than Walid.

"Blakeslee, I need you to be sure. Are you actually saying he put his hands on you?"

Silence.

"Blakeslee!"

"What are you going to do, Ace?"

"Did he hit you or not?"

"Yes, nigga! What!"

He was dizzy with rage. "Did you tell father?"

"He won't care."

"Father has his shit with him, but if he knew what Walid did, I'm sure he would get involved." He looked over at Arbella and down. "And then he had the audacity to do that right after he said what he said to me about my bitch."

"I don't want you to do anything."

"You know I can't promise you that."

"Please listen." She sniffled. "All I want to do is be with you. I don't want to live here anymore."

"When I get situated we will–"

"No! No more lies! You promised that once I was older that you would show me the world. That you would give me adventures. And I want what you promised otherwise, you a liar too!"

"Blakeslee, don't go there right now."

"Did you promise me these things or not?"

"You know I did. But things got dark over the past few months. You aren't even supposed to be talking to me on the phone. If father finds out he will cut you off too. Is that what you want?"

"Since when did you start caring about what father wants? You've always been a rebel. When are you going to stand up for me?"

"Don't go there."

"When I gave you that bracelet you said you would never take it off."

"And I haven't."

"But did you forget what the words said on it?"

Ace didn't forget.

But for the sake of the moment, he flipped the band on the bracelet and read under it. Etched in gold were the words, I SEE YOU.

"I see you." He said.

"Exactly. But I'm unable to do that right now. Because you feel so far away from me. It's supposed to be me and you against the world. Let me come, Ace. Please."

Ace was just about to respond when he saw a familiar face outside, staring from the window. He had two black eyes due to being punched in the nose.

Arbella spotted him too.

The wedding planner returned and said, "So I have the palettes for you to–."

"Wait a minute," she told him before moving to Ace. "That guy is back." She whispered while looking toward the window. "The one who kissed me."

"I see his ass." Ace's fist clenched and he hung up on Blakeslee.

"I promise I don't know who this person is."

He looked down at her and said, "I believe you. My father is involved. Walid probably involved too. And I know exactly what I'm going to do to them both. But first let me make this nigga know my name."

"Please don't go out there." She said, grabbing his hand.

"Stay right here." He snatched away and walked toward the door.

Strolling up to him Ace said, "I'm sorry about that shit in the restaurant."

He was shocked. "No worries. I just want you to know that she's lying to you. And playing mental games."

"For real?"

"Yes. We've been together for over a year. Talked about having children together and everything."

"Is that right?"

Before he could respond, Ace stole him in the face with the force of the blow knocking him on his back. Straddling him as if they were lovers, he hit him on the left of his face followed by a blow to the right.

Since the man had been summoned by Banks, the only thing he proceeded to do was get punched.

Luckily his brawn was not the purpose of his repeated visits. His sole purpose was to rattle his son's nerves and to sow doubt in his rocky relationship.

He succeeded.

Over and over he pounded the man's face until his arms lay outward at his sides with consciousness leaving his body slowly.

Ace hit him for not being able to be with his twin.

He hit him for the doubts he had successfully deposited in his mind about Arbella.

He struck him for Walid striking Blakeslee.

And he hit him for the hate brewing in his heart for his father.

He didn't stop striking him, until the wedding planner and Arbella pulled him away.

Virtually saving the man's life.

CHAPTER FOURTEEN
BANKS
"Meet me in the lounge in three minutes!"

Banks had a long night.

He also made a lot of strides that he hadn't prepared for with Kordell. Faye, the application designer, was not only experienced and knowledgeable, but she also provided additional advice that he was sure would help Kordell finally make his way into legit business.

But he would be dishonest if he didn't say he hadn't been thinking about her more often than not.

She was his style.

Young.

Smart.

Beautiful.

And driven.

There was also one thing that didn't allow Banks to ever get serious or hopeful when meeting women. And it was his transgender status. In his heart he was all man.

Always.

But would others feel the same?

It constantly hung over his head and in his mind, making it next to impossible to ever settle down.

When he walked into his kitchen to grab something to eat, he was shocked to see that most of the slices from the other boxes he ordered were gone. The Triad saw to that. But Blakeslee's small Hawaiian pizza, which only she enjoyed, was untouched.

This was odd because when he asked what she wanted to eat, she made a big deal of her order being a *certain way*.

Extra pineapple.

Extra pepperoni and three times as much sauce.

Lifting the lid, he saw a message written in red sauce.

Should Have Let Me Go.

Confused, Banks quickly rushed to her room to find out that her bed was made and she was gone. How had she gotten out? His house was flooded with guards. But sure enough, she was missing.

Enraged, he yelled down the corridors for everyone to wake up. Groggy and confused, they came to the door with eyes swollen with sleep.

"Meet me in the lounge in three minutes! Now!"

138

Everyone was present and that included Walid, Joey, Spacey and Mason. Minnesota was not there but since she was grieving, he gave her a pass. Although he was so mad, Walid had to remind him about her slain husband. The Triad was still asleep, but since they were too young to be involved in the family business, he didn't wake them.

More importantly his soldiers were there and it was them who he wanted to talk to the most.

They hung alongside the walls, each afraid that their lives as they knew it, would be over. Because Banks may have been demanding but he paid good money to protect his family and for the most part treated his men well.

If they didn't, however, he could be irrational.

If Blakeslee was gone, and she was, it meant they dropped the ball.

"Where is she?"

The security guards looked at one another, none really having an answer. The freak, who followed her in the bathroom that one time, spoke up. "I watched her like you told me to."

"You couldn't have." Mason interjected. "Otherwise, this meeting would be fruitless, and we would all be asleep."

"It's true. I watched her. But if she goes into the bathroom and hops out the window, there really is nothing I can do."

"Reminds me of Minnesota when she was young," Spacey whispered to Joey who agreed.

"I expect my daughter to be back here within the next few hours. If not, just like my family is disrupted at this moment, if she isn't returned, I will disrupt your families too."

LATER ON THAT NIGHT

Banks was in the office eating Blakeslee's pizza which he really didn't care for. But he needed something while he went over the events of the night. He was so scared she could place herself in harm's way, that he instructed not only the

By T. Styles

security guards, but also his sons to search for her whereabouts.

Most believed they knew where she was.

With Ace.

But no one wanted to say his name, since once again, Ace had taken a new address.

Another penthouse in Baltimore which meant he was off the map.

Banks took another bite when there was a soft knock at the door. "I'm busy."

"Father, it's me."

Surprised, he cleared his throat and said, "Come in, honey." He shuffled a few papers, in an attempt to tidy up.

Minnesota entered.

He rushed to help her to the chair and when she was seated, he sat and focused on her fully.

Her hair was combed, and she looked better than she had in the weeks prior despite the darkness under her eyes.

"Do you need anything, honey?"

"I'm not injured on the outside."

"I know. Still worried."

She smiled and breathed deeply. "I heard about Blakeslee."

He shook his head. "There was talk that her making an escape reminded everyone of you."

She laughed and it lit up his heart. "An escape? Finally admit it huh?"

He caught himself. "You know what I mean."

She nodded. "I know."

Her mood had been so dark that it was often difficult juggling what happened to her, in addition to managing his family. So lately he avoided her all together.

"Who said she reminds them of me? Spacey?"

"Probably."

"Well, it's true. I literally started the war. Me and Arlyndo."

"The past is over."

"How I wish that were true." She sighed and looked at him harder. "Are you okay, father?"

"You know what I want for this family. It's the same story in a different decade. And I don't understand why we can't stay together."

"She's young. We were too. And although you try to protect us from future danger, all we see is being fully protected. And that safety you provide makes us reckless."

He shook his head.

"Plus I think we try to push too hard to be the perfect family. When in reality we are what we are. Nothing more or less."

"Maybe you're right. But it won't change my mind. I'm getting us back to Wales Island."

"I know." She smiled. "You always do."

"I need to find a way to deal with Ace though. He's successfully maneuvering around Baltimore. I mean, where is he getting money from?"

"The girl?"

"Maybe, which is why I'm trying to get her away from him. And I have to admit, it's not my best work but still, I have to try something."

"Um...did I ever tell you what happened to me when great-grandmother locked Spacey and I in that attic?"

Banks moved a little uneasily. "No. But I guess I never asked."

The details were missed on Banks on purpose. Because he remembered that she and Spacey's relationship had grown unnatural in that dark place.

"Father, I think you need to listen to me. I have something very important to say. It will explain everything and may even help."

He leaned back and said, "I'm ready."

By T. Styles

CHAPTER FIFTEEN
WALID

"I guess I don't have a choice, do I?"

The dive bar smelled like old dirty carpet.

Because it was filled with old dirty carpeting.

Walid stood in front of the band who initially was responsible for getting Ace and he back to America.

The lead singer couldn't believe his request and at the same time due to going back and forth to Wales Island the men were wealthier than they had been in a long time.

And yet what he was asking now gave them chills.

The four members in the background allowed Number Five to do the talking for the group. "Does your father know about this request?"

"He doesn't have to know. The only thing important is will you help or not. Because the longer we stay here, the longer I see my family fall apart. Like now I'm supposed to be trying to find my little sister, and I don't know the first place to start. That's not going to happen to me or my wife."

The lead singer seemed uneasy but decided to speak anyway. "Your father was very angry with us for what happened. And in a way we felt used, especially after realizing Ace wasn't even a fan of our band. That it was all about leaving Belize."

The members shook their heads.

"And it wasn't even our fault. We had no idea that either of you were going to hide at the bottom of our plane and–."

"We both know what happened." Walid interrupted. "There's no getting around that. But this place is not for me. And it's not for my family." He stepped closer. "I need to leave. And I need you to help me."

"When are you trying to fly back out?"

"Tomorrow night."

"Even if the answer is yes, which I didn't say, we won't be able to do tomorrow night. We have a gig."

"I'm paying you enough money where you don't have to work for the rest of the year. Are you sure you want to deny my request?"

"We play music because we love it. Not for financial gain." He paused. "Why don't you rich people realize that? And can't you charter another jet?"

By T. Styles

Walid shook his head. "As you are aware, the island is off the grid. You have to know where you're going to find it. Which is why he paid you so much and made you sign a non-disclosure agreement before giving you the coordinates. I live there, but I don't even know what the coordinates are."

Number Five stepped closer. "I have no doubt that being the son of a billionaire allows you access to money we could never imagine. But your father has made some credible threats in the streets to anyone who aids his family in a way that goes against him. And people are listening. And people are afraid. So, taking you back home is not as simple as getting paid and calling it a day. There's so much more involved now."

Number Four stepped up. "Like I said we have to think about it. We're not saying no, but we aren't saying yes either."

Walid was angry.

Since he came back to the States for the brief time that they had been there, he took a few courses in flying. But he wasn't a natural like Spacey or his father.

In other words, it would be a long time before he felt comfortable chartering a plane on his own.

"I guess I don't have any choice, do I?"

At first Walid thought Ace was going to set him up but per plan, at midnight, he showed up.

Ace had a smile on his face and there was a twinkle of deviousness in his eyes. What he also noticed was his bruised hands.

Walid rushed up to him. "Ain't no need in playing games. Where is she?"

"Oh, you talking about little sis?" He said pointing at him.

"I told you what this was about over the phone."

"I guess I forget what you say sometimes, Walid. You aren't a priority anymore."

Walid looked down and back at him. "I'm trying to talk to you. Brother to brother. But you're making this difficult. Why would you even get her mixed up in all this anyway?"

"I thought we weren't brothers no more."

"Ace."

"And what you mean why did I get her mixed up? I made it clear from the jump that I wanted no parts of living on that island. And yet father can't seem to leave me alone. You think he hears me now?"

"What you're doing is going to hurt Blakeslee in the long run." He pointed at the ground.

"I'm her brother. What's safer than me? Besides, you the one who hit her." Now his expression turned dark and for the first time Walid felt fear for his life. "Why you do that, twin?"

"I didn't hit her."

"I saw her face."

"I would never hurt my little sister on purpose. It was an accident. Which started because of what I saw on her phone."

"What you talking about?"

Always the protector of secrets, he said, "That's irrelevant. Like I said, it was an accident and at the same time she needs to be with us. If you want to be alone out here that's one thing, but don't drag her into all this shit."

Ace moved closer. "I know Joey sent that dude to fuck with me and my girl. I beat the truth out of him."

"I don't know what you're talking about."

"My thing is this...even if my gripe is with father, y'all niggas can't help but take his side."

"That ain't what I'm here to talk about."

"This family has never respected or even liked me. Ever!"

"Where is she, man?"

"Joey should have never gotten my girl involved, Walid. Father never should have gotten my girl involved. Everything that happens from this point on is on y'all." He pointed his way.

"The thing is, niggas are starting to not give a fuck about you no more. And I can't wait. Because when that happens, we will be long gone."

"I see the look in your eyes." Ace paused. "I can tell the hate you have for me. And it's sad."

Walid laughed.

"I left something for Joey at home."

Walid's smile disappeared. "What is that supposed to mean?"

"It's a gift, brother. A gift that will free him. A gift that will finally free me too." He turned to walk away. "And don't bother trying to find me. I have people watching my back as we speak."

Suddenly 10 men stepped from the background.

They worked for Aliyah's father, but at the moment their allegiance was to Ace.

CHAPTER SIXTEEN
WALID
"If you going to tell me the story, tell me everything, Joey."

Walid was in the car with Joey on the way to his house.

As they waited, he could see the pain in Joey's eyes, and he regretted telling him that Ace had alluded to trouble in his home. At the same time, he felt he needed to prepare him for whatever Ace had in store.

"Did she answer your call yet?" Walid asked, glancing from the passenger's seat.

"Nope."

"There is always a possibility that he's just talking shit. You know that right?"

"I don't trust him. I never have. So I think this threat is credible."

"Not like we need a reason, but why don't you trust him?"

"You're probably too young to remember but there's always been a darkness surrounding Ace. Originally everybody thought you would be the one who would wreak havoc, but it soon became clear who the monster in this family really was."

Walid scratched his scalp and dropped his hand in his lap. "We had everything in Belize. And now I can't help but think that we are about to have nothing."

"Look at it this way. The best thing that came out of this is the fact that you are your own man now."

"What does that mean?"

"You no longer out here trying to protect that nigga. Your focus seems to be on yourself and your family."

"I definitely placed the line in the sand with Ace. But he's going to always be my brother. Always my twin." He looked out the window. "And that's what makes this hurt so bad. If I could only understand why he moves the way he does then maybe—"

"Are you ready for me to tell you everything?"

He frowned. "Everything like what?"

"How you came to be."

Walid moved a little uneasily. "I'm listening."

"Back in the day, pops started dating Mason's wife."

"That's foul."

By T. Styles

"I still don't understand how that happened. Still, there was a brief period where everybody felt like pops and Jersey were really in love. And people believed that Mason never cared for Jersey in the first place. That she was always a placemat for someone else."

"Someone else, like who?"

Silence.

"If you going to tell me the story, tell me everything, Joey."

"I don't proclaim to know all the details. But by now I hope you understand that pops was born a girl. His dead name is Blakeslee."

"So he has to hear his dead name every day?"

"What you mean?"

"Uh, our sister's name is Blakeslee too."

He shook his head. "Never thought about it until now. It's probably why pops and Blakeslee don't get along. And from what I hear she looks just like pops back in the day. Now that I think about it, I believe calling her that was Jersey's idea."

Walid shook his head feeling bad for Banks.

"Anyway, back in the day when he was female, Mason loved her. And he always held on to that love despite my father not being who he wanted him to be. So when I say Jersey was a placemat, I'm telling you she was a placement for pops. And we all believe Mason still loves him to this day."

It was all too confusing. "So how did you come to be? And Minnesota? And Spacey?"

"I'm told so many things. To make it easier just know that your blood is not the same as Spacey's or mine. But Minnesota is your blood sister. Because just like he used his eggs for you and Ace to be born, he did the same for Minnesota and Blakeslee."

"I don't give a fuck. We still brothers."

"Facts."

Walid took in a deep breath. "This shit needs to be on a TV show."

"Like I said, it's all complicated."

"That's an understatement."

"So, when pops was with Jersey, Mason learned that they were in a relationship behind his back, and that they were planning children together. So he inserted his sperm into the process, instead of the chosen donor. That action merged pops and Mason's blood lines together resulting in you and Ace. Jersey carried both of you to full term."

Walid, for the first time understood what was happening.

154   By T. Styles

But he was suddenly worried.

"Why are you telling me this right now?"

Joey parked outside of his house and looked at the window. He could see Sydney's silhouette moving about their home. "Because I don't know what's about to happen. And if something happens to me, I wanted what we agreed about months back to be explained to you."

Walid nodded slowly.

They exited the car and walked up to Joey's house.

Surprisingly enough unlike in the past when they opened the door Sydney was singing happily about the living room. It wasn't until Joey walked up to her that she was frightened.

"What are you doing here?" She asked.

He glared. "What you mean what I'm doing here? This my crib. Paid for in cash."

"I mean, I thought you were staying at the other house." She looked at Walid. "Hey, Walid."

He nodded.

"Ace been in here?" Joey asked.

Silence.

He stepped closer. "Has Ace been in my house?"

Suddenly tears streamed down her face. "He...he told you?"

"Told me what?"

"Joey, maybe we should go." Walid said.

"Hold up...you...you fucked my brother?"

"It wasn't like that." She sobbed harder. "You wouldn't talk to me. You wouldn't hold me. You wouldn't do anything."

"So you let him come over here and disrespect me tonight? When you know he's been causing us problems?"

"Tonight?" She sniffled and wiped the tears away. "Ace didn't come over here tonight."

Joey was confused. "Did you fuck my brother or not?"

"He was there for me when I needed him and–"

"Answer the question!"

She looked down. "I have always been in love with you, Joey. But I'm realizing that you and your family are so dead set on treating people like property. It's like you all are playwrights and you cast us as actors. If someone doesn't fulfill a role you just toss them out and it's not right! It's not right!"

"Did you fuck him or not!"

"I'm pregnant!" She yelled. "That's why I'm gaining weight. And it happened when Ace and

By T. Styles

Walid first came into town." She flopped on the sofa. "You all were out on the patio. And I had just brought out tea and you were so mean to me. But he saw me. Even smiled at me and the next day, invited me out. It meant nothing because we had sex in the car but...but...I thought you knew."

"So he had been in town for less than a week and you went there?"

She nodded yes as huge tears fell from her eyes. "But I tried to kill the baby. Which is why I drank so much. But then guilt would consume me and when I checked with the doctors, the following day, they'd always say he was well."

"A boy?" Joey whispered.

She wiped tears away.

"Joey, let's go," Walid begged.

He rushed toward her and Walid stopped him from laying hands. But with the strength only an older brother possessed, he grabbed him by his shoulders and shook hard. "Go outside and wait for me, Walid."

"I can't let you hurt her."

"Go outside!" He breathed heavily. "I won't say it again."

Reluctantly he did as his older brother requested.

It took some time but eventually he heard screams followed by silence within the walls.

Sweating...

And mostly out of breath....

Joey returned to the car.

Staring straight ahead from the passenger seat he said, "What happened here is between us."

"You really gotta say that to me?" Walid asked.

Joey smiled. "Nah. You always been solid." He looked back at his house. "She's right about one thing though."

"What's that?"

"We do cast people in and out of our lives." He looked at him. "And for the first time ever I'm starting to realize we the villains. And that whatever happens to us, we deserve."

"Is she okay?"

"I don't know. But I seriously doubt she'll be having a baby. Unless that little nigga made of stone." He took a deep breath. "Drive. I'm ready to go home."

CHAPTER SEVENTEEN
ACE
"I'm not my father!"

Ace met with Mr. Valentine alone in his library within his penthouse.

When Ace took a seat, he was enamored with all the books on the wall. "You read all of these?" He wiped wild curls from his eyes.

Proudly he said, "Every single one. Quite a few of them with Arbella. It's our pastime." He paused. "Well before you forbid her to see me it used to be."

"Thank you for allowing me to use your men. But why did you help me? Because I still don't think you should be around her right now."

"I helped you because you asked."

"There has to be another reason."

He sat deeply in his chair. "There will come a time in the future where I may need your help. And I may have to call on you. My only request is that you remember today."

"I'm not my father."

"But you're still a Wales! The name alone has power and you don't even realize it! Surely living in luxury hasn't made you clueless to the fact that people would kill to be in your shoes."

"You don't get it." He stood up and walked across the room. "I'm trying to escape from all that shit. I want to live my own life. And not have to worry about being subject to his rules just because he has money."

His brows lowered. "You sound foolish."

Ace glared.

"Like I said, you are in a position most would die to be in. But the handicap you have of never knowing what life is like on the other side doesn't allow you to see your blessings. In the real-world people have to think about how to take care of themselves first and the people they care for second. Money always seems to be an ongoing issue for us and it makes for a very uncomfortable existence. But you have the benefit of having both money and power and you hate your father for it?"

"I can do things myself."

"Well, whose money are you using now? Whose name do you bear? You can't even begin to separate yourself if you keep the same name!"

"You don't know me."

"I helped you tonight because you were concerned your father might show up when your

160

brother wanted to meet. I helped you because you are Ace Wales."

"Fuck are you trying to say?"

"Son, let me make this plain. I'm in need. And had you not been a Wales I would have never allowed your yellow ass to have access to my men, or to even step foot in my home. Now that's power. You still wanna leave?"

Ace was sitting on the sofa with Blakeslee as Arbella was in the kitchen preparing dinner.

Arbella was so excited that he went to see her father that she was floating around the kitchen and humming. They still weren't allowed to speak, but at least there was the possibility that they would all be family in the future in her mind.

While Blakeslee, on the other hand, was doing her level best to get his attention.

"I'm so happy you came back for me, brother. Nobody else understands me and what it's like living with father." She played with the bracelet on his arm. "You kept your promise, and I will never forget it."

"I told you I would come back for you. I just wish I had more time. Because this place is nice, but it's not it for me. I want bigger."

"But more time to do what?" She got up and danced around the sofa before flopping next to him again as if she were acting in a play. "This is freedom! Up high! That makes it heaven!"

"We aren't living where I want to live in the long run, Blakeslee. And I'm still using the money I got from father. When it's all gone, I don't have another plan yet. So shit is not in stone."

"Oh, silly! You're fine! We are both going to be fine. Isn't that right, Arbella?"

"You're including me? Because you said *both* and not the *three* of us."

Blakeslee rolled her eyes. "Anyway, Ace, let me show you the picture of my boyfriend." She removed a new phone from her pocket that Ace purchased for her and showed him the screen. "Isn't he perfect?"

What did she want him to say? He wasn't into dudes. "He's all right."

"Don't be jealous, brother. I haven't done it yet, but I bet he gives the best kisses ever."

162

He shot his head in her direction. "I don't want you having sex with anybody. You know that right?"

"Oh, pew! I would never! But I can tell that he can kiss." The thing was she thought about sex every minute of every day, despite being a virgin.

"Well since you haven't kissed anybody, you'll only kiss somebody when the time is right. And that time is not now."

"I can't wait until I turn eighteen to find out."

"Blakeslee, stop being fresh." Arbella said as she stirred spaghetti sauce in the pot. "You're still a little girl."

Blakeslee was incensed. "Why would you call me that around my brother?"

"Because you are acting loose."

"Well I'm not. And you should be careful about the things you say to me."

"If you're going to live with us, there will still be rules. I won't let some little girl–."

"Did you tell my brother you fucked Walid?"

Arbella accidentally knocked the pot of sauce to the floor. It splattered everywhere like a crime scene.

"What did you just say?" He asked his sister.

Blakeslee smiled sinisterly. "She had sex with Walid! Tell him! Since you're so concerned about people being fresh... *little girl*."

Ace rose slowly.

Wanting to get it all over, Arbella walked toward him. "I didn't know it was him."

He lowered his head. "So it's true?"

"Yes."

He dragged her toward the balcony and Blakeslee opened the door, hanging her halfway over he said, "Tell me why I shouldn't drop you right now!"

One false move and she would've toppled and splashed to her death.

"Ace, please don't! I'm begging you!"

"What happened?"

Blakeslee danced on the balcony happily as she waited for the results.

"It was when you were missing! They tried to get information out of me about my father and Lance's whereabouts! So Walid pretended to be you!" She cried harder and was barely audible over the bustling city. "I guess they figured the only way to do it was to convince me that he was you! Please don't hurt me!"

"So you're telling me you slept with my brother? My twin? No wonder he was so concerned about you. He had been in that pussy!" Tears streamed down his face and for the first time despite dangling, Arbella could see sincere pain in his eyes.

"Ace, I'm so, so sorry. But I'm begging you...please don't let me go."

CHAPTER EIGHTEEN
WALID
"Joey explained everything."

Spacey was sitting on the lawn overlooking the garden. When Walid walked out he could tell he was deep in thought. "You been drinking?" Walid asked.

"No, father." Spacey said jokingly. "Ain't been in the mood for the last couple of days." He took a deep breath. "Any word on Blakeslee?"

"Nah. You found out anything?"

"Nope." Spacey readjusted. "Pops is heated too."

"I get it. We dropped the ball big time." He looked down and back at Spacey. "Can you do me a favor?"

"Depends."

"Show me your wings."

An hour later they were in the skies.

Walid sat in the cockpit next to him amazed at how effortlessly he flew the aircraft. He wanted to see his wings to learn what was possible for him in the future. He only hoped to someday be just as good but for now all he could do was push a few buttons on the control panel.

"How did you get so good?"

"Well in the beginning this was the only way I could connect with pops. He loves flying so much that I took to it to link with him. To get closer." He paused. "I don't know how much you know, but we aren't his blood children."

"Yeah, I got the deets. Joey explained everything."

"Thank God."

Walid laughed.

"So, how your flying classes been coming along?"

"I'm not picking up on it the way that I want." Walid admitted.

"Explain."

"I don't know." He shrugged. "It's just not happening for me quick or smoothly enough. I'm almost about to give up."

"That's because you're rushing it, little brother. When you fly you have to respect the process. You have to respect nature. And you have to respect the skies. If you don't have balance, then flying won't become a part of you. It needs to become a part of you first."

Walid took a deep breath. He could admit to himself that he was definitely pushing it hard, mainly because he wanted to go home so badly.

"You're struggling here, aren't you?" Spacey probed.

"You don't know the half." Walid said honestly.

"I'll take you home."

Walid was almost dizzy from his response. Partially because he hadn't expected it. And also because he hadn't thought to ask him in the first place. He assumed that just like Joey, he would do everything Banks said.

And Banks wanted everyone to stay together.

If one was on the island, all were on the island.

"But what about father?"

"Do you remember when great-grandmother had me and Minnesota in that attic?"

"I remember. I remember everything. Even feeding and talking to you through the door."

"I felt trapped. I wasn't eating. There was no outside line of communication for me. Until you. And I know that doing this for you may put a wedge between me and pops, but I feel like I owe you. If this will make you happy you can consider it done. And if you spend more time with me, I'll also teach you how to fly."

168   **By T. Styles**

Walid wrapped his arms around his neck and Spacey laughed as he continued to handle the blue skies.

———✈———

Walid spent one of the best times he ever had in life with his older brother on the aircraft and he couldn't wait to tell Aliyah the great news. Thanks to Spacey, they no longer had to wait until everything blew over with his father's business associates or Ace.

Due to Walid's good nature as a child and being there for Spacey when he was in the attic with Minnesota so many years ago, he was flying them home.

Excited about the good news, when he opened his bedroom door Aliyah was standing in front of him with bloodshot red eyes. He could tell she'd been crying and without words he knew exactly what went down.

She found out about him killing her father.

This was the one thing he dreaded all those years ago. That she would eventually discover that

THE GODS OF EVERYTHING ELSE 2   169

she'd unknowingly bedded the man who shifted her life. How he wished he told her before.

But how do you tell someone that you love more than anything, that you did such a permanent thing?

"You fucked Arbella?" She asked, wiping her tears away.

Relief washed over him.

Even though sleeping with Arbella was bad too, this was something he was certain he could wiggle out of with a little work and a few dick strokes. And if he did, it would be more important than ever to get his family away before Ace snitched again.

He stepped closer. "Baby..."

"Don't baby me!"

He stopped walking.

"Answer the fucking question, Walid! Did you fuck her or not?"

He looked downward.

It was best to come clean than to remain dirty.

"It was the only way she would tell me information about her father or where Lance was at the time. We thought Ace was hurt. And we needed information. She alone had the details. She wouldn't tell us anything any other way, Aliyah. You have to believe me." A hand over his heart.

By T. Styles

"If that was the only reason, why didn't you tell me? Why did you leave it for Ace to bring it to my attention? Do you know how painful this shit is? Do you know how much I'm hurting? He threw it in my face as a way to say I made a mistake when I chose you."

Still relieved that Ace hadn't revealed the secret about her father, Walid knew full well the man was in the snitching mood, which was all the more reason to leave Baltimore for good.

"This on me, baby."

"Tell me something I don't know."

He stepped closer. "But I promise you she means nothing. It doesn't make things better, I know. But it's still the truth."

"It sure doesn't."

"But I need to let you know this...I only did it for Ace. But I'm done with his selfish ass."

"So why didn't you tell me? You still haven't given me a reason."

A soft hand to the middle of her back with a pull closer. "I wanted to. But you were so adamant about not destroying our relationship that I buckled." Another hand to the small of her back. "Do you forgive me?"

"No."

He tugged her closer and kissed her cheek "Please, baby."

"Stop." Her tone was soft as her defenses broke down.

He kissed her lips. "I'm begging you."

"Walid, is there anything else I don't know? Because I can't have him keep coming to me and hurting my heart the way he does. You know he never got over me choosing you. He really is a monster."

He thought about her father and chose not to tell her at the moment.

"Nothing." He kissed her forehead, neck and then her breasts. "And I'll do anything that you want. Just please don't leave me."

He lowered his height and tugged at her black tights, tossing them across the room.

"Walid, no..." she whispered.

He pushed down her panties and tapped her inner right thigh and then the left, which forced her to assume the position.

With both hands on her ass cheeks, he slithered his tongue toward her clit. Her body pulsated. Wanting to taste her more, he pushed into her tunnel, collecting more juice as he suckled softly on her button.

172   By T. Styles

"Walid..." she moaned.

Guiding her legs over his shoulders, he picked her up with his tongue never leaving her pussy. Up high, close to the ceiling, her back was against the wall, as he suckled and licked her pussy so much, she was dripping wet.

Grinding into his face, she felt herself on the verge. "Walid..."

He was silent.

Besides, he was busy.

"Wa...Walid."

"Yes, baby."

"Do to me what you did to her. And then maybe I'll forgive you."

He looked up at her and softly put her down.

"Are you sure?"

"Fuck me like you fucked her."

Standing on her own two feet, he led her to the bed. With his back against the headboard, he removed his dick and stroked it to a complete thickness.

"Get the fuck over here."

One leg to the left of him. One leg to the right of him. And before she knew it she was stuffed full of dick.

Next he removed his French Braids and allowed his hair to fall over his head until curls covered his eyes.

Her body tingled as she bared witness to Ace. Slamming her lips against his, she moved up and down as their sex session grew erotic, passionate, and somewhat violent as he thrust into her without care for pain.

In the end, he exploded into her pussy while looking into her eyes.

Out of breath, tears in her eyes and totally satisfied she said, "Forgiven."

By T. Styles

CHAPTER NINETEEN
BANKS

"Do you choose me or him?"

Banks, Mason, and Kordell sat in the boardroom going over his new app.

Unlike in the past, Kordell seemed excited about what he was seeing. With the help of Faye, they created an app that showcased one outfit, side by side, being worn by two separate people. There was not only a side by side set up for clothing, but also for hairstyles too.

But what made this app successful was that advertisers would place money into the application to have their clothing showcased. While influencers would gain notoriety due to people liking their display choices of the clothing over another.

It was a run of the mill rating system, but it was brilliant.

To ensure it would pop off, Banks redirected Kordell's funds to hire one hundred of the most popular influencers in the world. For over a month they went about talking about *the next big thing*.

With the first release being invite only, people signed up to the waiting list in droves, wondering who would be accepted and who wouldn't.

After its official launch, Kordell saw one million dollars in pure profit. If the pace continued, which by all accounts it would, he would legitimately be seen as a businessman instead of a dope dealer.

In the beginning he would be washing money.

In the end he would be out of the game totally.

"I have to admit, I didn't see this going through." Kordell said.

"I know it's not titties but with the amount of money you're making this just as pretty."

"If not prettier!" Kordell placed his fist over his mouth and laughed heartily. "I hate to admit it but helping you single-handedly was one of the best decisions I ever made in my life. And if you need anything else in the future let me know." He placed a hand over his cocaine heart.

Banks thought about the rough start they had getting the app to launch but remembered his services in Mexico. "Look, you killing Nicolas and allowing us to get out of there was all I needed."

He looked down and back at him. "I'm serious, Banks, anything you need I got you with my whole life."

By T. Styles

"I think we good." Mason interjected.

Kordell laughed. "One of these days I'm going to grow on you, Mason."

"I'll believe it when I see it."

They continued to look over the different features of his new app, which was simply called *The Kordell,* when Banks received an unusual call from his Banker. "Give me a second. I have to answer this."

Unlike in the past, Kordell didn't contest. After all, Banks had been good on his word, and done everything he promised.

Standing in the corner he accepted the call. "If you're hitting me up, it means something popped off with my money. So what is it?"

"Sir, I think you should come to the US office and speak with me at once."

He glared. "Nah, tell me what's up now."

"Well, I was able to look at your year-end statements and noticed a disturbing trend I hadn't seen before."

"I'm waiting."

"Minute levels of money have been disappearing from your accounts to another account for months and even years."

He glared. "I don't understand what you're telling me."

"Someone has been stealing from you."

"How is that possible? I go over my accounts monthly with you. I haven't seen any substantial amount of funds being taken. Ever!"

"This was the ingenuity of the entire thing. Because they were low-level amounts that could be overlooked at first. Recently however, the amounts went higher so whoever is responsible has gotten more brazen."

"How did you find out?"

"I installed a new system that goes back five years. And it was all there before my eyes. The recent amounts I'm surprised you didn't detect. It's been upwards of thousands a month. I need permission to change your banking account numbers to stop them in their tracks."

Banks had been so busy with bringing Ace back that he didn't go over his affairs anymore. "Do it."

He heard clicking in the background. "Done."

"Now, how much are we talking?"

"Just in the time you've been in the states alone, they have stolen two million. For a total of close to twelve million dollars."

Banks almost blacked out.

By T. Styles

Mason rose upon seeing the look of rage on his friend's face. "What's going on, Banks?"

"Do you know who's responsible?" He breathed heavily, focusing on the call.

"We traced the bank and–."

"Who the fuck is stealing from me?!" He roared.

"It appears to be your son." A deep breath. "Ace."

Banks ended the call and made another. "Put a picture out on the streets for my son. I need him brought to me. Now!"

"Is there any particular way?"

"As long as he's alive, bruised will do."

"Understood."

Mason dragged a hand down his face and walked away.

Banks was sitting in his office two days later with no more information on Ace or his whereabouts then he had in the beginning. Not only that, but Ace drained the account used to transfer the stolen funds thereby putting the money somewhere else.

He underestimated his son greatly.

He didn't know him to be a thief. And yet there was all the proof in the world right before his eyes. Being virtually a stranger in America, he didn't ask for a single dollar since he'd been in the states.

In fact, Banks assumed his need for money would be the first thing to make him return to the Wales Way.

But it hadn't and now he knew why.

Mason walked into his office. "What's happening now?" He leaned against the wall. The Baltimore air appeared to restore him because he barely used his cane most days.

"If you want to ask me something, be direct. You know I prefer it that way."

"What are your plans for my son?"

"He stole from me, Mason."

"If it was such a big deal you would have felt the sting before. You're a billionaire."

"Does that give him the right to violate my trust? At the end of the day it's not about money. But to know that a snake this vicious is born of my blood...I...all I know is he's not getting away with it!"

By T. Styles

"I warned you that this could get out of hand!" He yelled. "And yet if you continue to push, I see the worst happening!"

"Lower your voice!"

Mason rushed toward him and shoved all the papers off his desk. They floated to the floor like snow. "I'm not your fucking child! You will respect me; I swear to God!"

Banks stood up and the two breathed heavily in front of one another.

The wrong thing said could be final.

In Mason, Banks met his match.

Mason took a deep breath.

Banks reclaimed his seat.

"I think you need to slow down." Mason continued, stepping back. "I think we all need to slow down. Let the boy have the money. Let's go back to the island. When he's run through it, and he will, the lines of communication will reopen. I'm begging you, man."

"I'm beyond that now."

"What about what that will do to us?" Mason pleaded.

Banks looked up at him. "What are you saying?"

"He's my son and as wicked as he is I...I see myself in him. And I can see in your eyes that whatever you have planned may hurt him."

"Mason, I—."

"Are you gonna hurt my son?"

Banks took a deep breath. "We've been doing life together at this point longer than any relationship I ever had. Literally, we have seen and gone through everything together."

"True," Mason nodded.

"So let me be quick. Do you choose me or him?"

Silence.

"Mason...I need an answer!"

He took a deep breath. "You. Always you." He stormed out, punching the wall in the process.

CHAPTER TWENTY
ACE
"Would you prefer a lie?"

A ce forgave Arbella.

In his mind, she alone was the reason for everything he was doing, even despite the betrayal. Still, he had them relocated to their new penthouse in a ritzy part of Washington D.C.

After he was certain that it became clear that he impregnated Sydney, he was sure that the family would stop at nothing to get back at him. Moving was more important than ever because Arbella didn't know about the baby. Add to the pressure the fact that out of vengeance, he told Aliyah about Arbella.

Heat would be coming soon, he was certain.

It would be easy to break down his home because tension was growing in his own relationships.

For starters, Blakeslee didn't like Arbella and the feeling was mutual. They argued daily about the most mundane things, which often forced him out of the house.

But he was also unsure about his girl.

After learning about her sexual encounter with Walid, and wondering if she liked it, his mind ran rampant with crazy thoughts. He had even gone as far as to put a tracker on her car, but whenever she would venture into certain parts of town, it seemed to disconnect.

This frustrated him even more.

But he loved her. And when they were together she went overboard to show him how much she cared and how sorry she was about Walid. It took many days and hours filled with long talks. But it finally made sense.

How could Arbella, who just met Ace at the time, tell him apart from a twin brother she didn't even know he had?

They were walking down the block from their new apartment which was located in a part of town that had shops, eateries, and cute boutiques to buy clothing. Every now and again he would look at her beauty and fear would rise in him.

He couldn't lose her.

He was by all accounts, obsessed.

She was his sole reason for wanting everything so without her he would have nothing. How could he calm a mind that moved in extremes without scaring her away? He needed her to know he was capable of great things, but love was also the driving force to his actions.

She was his entire world.

He wrapped an arm around her neck like a scarf. "Where were you today?"

She shrugged. "Just went driving."

They walked around a couple kissing and he fake smiled, believing that's what *regular* people do. "Why do you continuously lie to me, Arbella?"

"I hate that you think that about me. I think the issue we have is trust."

"And whose fault is that? Mine or yours?"

Walid's name was in the air despite neither saying the word.

"It's all me, Ace." A deep breath filled her chest cavity. "But you said you forgave me. Did you really? Because if you don't, this won't work. I would have never gone there with your brother had I known it was not you."

"You know, you said that before..."

She looked at him and back ahead. "Said what?"

"That it won't work. At this point we're stuck together. Forever. So you have no choice. You either be with me or I'll kill you and the nigga you with."

"Ace!"

"Would you prefer a lie?"

"You have to stop being so intense."

"If something happened to me, your world would be rocked. And you can't even see it."

She took a deep breath. "Do you believe I want Walid? I need to know because I can't be afraid that you will snap."

"I told you before, I believe you. Walid has always wanted what belongs to me. And I don't see that changing anytime soon."

Suddenly two men walked behind them. They were speaking in Spanish, and because Walid and Ace spoke over ten languages fluently, he understood every word said.

Clearly.

"*That's him. That's the one in the photo*," One of the men whispered. "*Let's grab him before he gets away*."

Ace pulled Arbella to him and kissed her passionately. Then he whispered in her ear, "Run."

"What are you–."

He grabbed her so tightly again, he almost choked the air from her lungs. "I said run, Arbella. Now."

Without another word, she took off in one direction and he went in another to lead them away from her. He would be shaken if something happened to his girl.

When they finally stopped running, they were in a virtually empty garage.

"Who are you?" Ace asked mostly out of breath, looking between the two strangers for answers.

They spoke in Spanish, mainly talking to each other. "*When I give the word you move on the right and I'll take the left.*"

"*I said who are you and what do you want with me?*" Ace said in very fluent Spanish.

The lead person said, "*You understand us?*"

"*Every word.*"

"*Then understand this, you are coming with us.*"

"*Who sent you?*"

"*Why does it matter? You are only delaying the inevitable.*"

"*I'm going to make this clear. I'm not going anywhere. With you or anybody else. I'm also sure the person who sent you said to grab me alive. May the last one standing win.*"

CHAPTER TWENTY-ONE
BANKS
"If only it had been just Walid."

Thunder and rain pounded the earth.

Pacing in his office, Banks was getting frustrated that he hadn't heard anything about Ace or Blakeslee.

Did they get him or didn't they?

Part of the predicament he was in was that he didn't have anybody he trusted at his side who was deeply connected to the streets anymore. This left him relying on new niggas to do family business.

The ones he *did* trust...Mason, Spacey, Joey and Walid were all out trudging the streets to find them too. He even put his hired hands on the blocks while Minnesota went to the store to get some fresh air and groceries to make dinner. Although the hood life was no longer in her soul, she wanted to do something to help.

Only one man stayed behind, refusing to leave him alone and he manned the front door.

When his phone rang he rushed toward it and quickly answered an unrecognizable number. "Where is he?"

By T. Styles

"Father, can we talk?"

He took a deep breath.

It was Ace.

"Where is Blakeslee?"

"With me. And she's safe but she's not coming home right now."

He shook his head. "Where are you?"

"Not too far from your house. I know you're looking for me. I figured I'd bring myself to make things easier. Because the way things have been going, now I'm scared."

Banks smiled. "So you realize that shit ain't a game no more huh?"

"Yes, father. And I don't know what got into me. I should have never challenged you the way I did. Please, can we talk?"

"Pull up and my man will let you inside."

"I'll be there in 5 minutes."

When Ace finally walked into the office, Banks was slightly taken aback by the fresh and old scars on his face. The old scars settled upon his skin like weird imperfections. Coupled with the new bruises, his darkness shined through.

In a sense, Banks didn't recognize his own son.

He didn't look...

Well.

Banks sat behind his desk and motioned for him to take a seat.

He did.

"You stole from me."

"That's what this is about? You're a billionaire, father. Surely that amount of money didn't put you in a bind."

"It's still my money. And I gave you more than you could spend. More than you needed in your own personal accounts. Why take from me?"

"You mean the accounts you cut off?"

"They are yours if you return home. Even now."

"Out there I'm already home."

"What is wrong with you, son? I don't understand. My only crime is that I've given you everything that you ever desired and yet you–"

"How do you know what I desired? You never stopped to ask me! You just assumed I wanted diamonds and money." Tears welled up in his eyes. "When it was about so much more to me."

"Like what?"

"Time! And a...a mother who–."

At the mere mention of being female Banks snapped. "I was never supposed to be your fucking mother!" He beat his chest. "That's the entire point!

I was sick and suffered a brain injury which momentarily fucked up my life!"

"So you didn't want me?"

"I never said that! Every single one of my kids were planned." He pointed at the floor. "From Spacey all the way down to Blakeslee. But the picture was different in my mind. And if you weren't so spoiled, you would see that! You would see me!"

Ace shook his head.

"You are worried about things that don't matter, Ace. You think I had a mother who was always there for me?"

"Father, all I'm saying is that at one point it was just me, Walid, and you. And those are the best memories I ever had in my life. And then Mason and the others came and she...you...were gone." Tears fell harder. "I miss you. I miss the three of us."

Banks stood up from the desk and shoved his file cabinet that sat in the corner. His breathing was heavy and erratic, and he felt what he hadn't in some time.

A panic attack.

"I will not allow you to make this about me." He pointed at him. "Do you hear me? This is about you! Look at the jewels around your neck! That's because of me."

"And I would give up everything," He raised the chain and allowed it to fall upon his chest. "...all of it, for a dime."

"If only it had been just Walid."

That hurt.

Badly.

"I'm pouring my heart out and you still can't hear me." Ace said softly.

Banks looked at the window. In a low but steady voice he said, "You don't know what it's like to struggle. I grew up in an environment where safety was a luxury. Where food was not daily. There were times when I didn't know if I would have to take care of myself because my mother was mentally unstable and my father was not available." He turned to face him. "Say what you want about me but I was always there for my kids!" He pointed at the floor. "Always!"

"You...you actually forgot?"

"What are you talking about now?" Banks said, pacing in small circles with his hands on his hips.

"For a while you left us alone. With Mason and the others. And none of them, not a one, loved me like you used to."

192   By T. Styles

Banks recalled a brief moment in his life when he bounced but surely that wasn't enough for him to lose his mind.

"I needed to regroup."

"But when you returned, you were not the same. You were male. You didn't even sit down and explain everything. I don't even know...I don't even know how I came to be."

"I...I had to get myself together. But when I returned, I stepped up and provided a life where you would never have to worry. Because I didn't want any of my children to experience the type of fear I did growing up in Baltimore."

"But that's life. Fear. All of it."

"Says the boy who lived in luxury on a private island."

"You're so set on getting rid of the person you were when you lived in Baltimore that you never stopped to think what I wanted. Or Walid. Or Spacey and them. Why does everything have to be about the bad?"

"Again, says the boy who lived in luxury all of his life."

Ace took a deep breath.

It was no use.

Banks' mind was set.

"You should have left me alone. That was a major mistake because you, my dear father, literally came too close to the son."

"Too close to the son? Are you...are you threatening me?"

Suddenly there was heavy activity in the distance.

Sirens and noise screamed outside of the house.

Banks looked at Ace trying to understand what was happening. Within seconds his only man guarding the door entered.

"The police are here." He said with a heavy breath.

"For what?"

"I don't know, sir. They have a warrant and it doesn't look good."

"Well let them in. I haven't done anything wrong."

When he was gone Ace said, "Are you sure about that?"

He glared. "What are you talking about?"

"I'm just the boy who lived in luxury all his life, but I seem to remember a kidnapping from a facility when I was a child. Grant it you are my father but when you took me from the State of

By T. Styles

Maryland you broke the law. Maybe...I don't know, somehow the police found out." He grinned wider.

"Wait, you called the cops on me about that?"

Before he could refute the police busted through his home. Banks could hear them trashing the place because of the sound of broken glass and furniture and he wondered why.

When it seemed like forever, and after causing major destruction in his estate, they finally entered his office.

"Are you Banks Wales?" The lead detective questioned. Hate was etched all over her face.

He couldn't speak.

His son had broken his heart.

The pain he experienced in that moment due to Ace's betrayal weighed upon him like huge boulders. They may have had their beef but he never, ever, thought he would stoop so low.

"Are you Banks Wales?" The officer said louder.

"He is." Ace answered for him.

"I know he is," she said through clenched teeth. "I remember that smug face from the newspaper. Banks the Billionaire. A Baltimore Sensation. I also remember two friends of mine, both officers who are still missing to this day. And how your friends Mason and Jersey Louisville were likely responsible."

"W...what?" Banks muttered.

"You used your money to make the situation go away. But I know they had something to do with their disappearances."

"Who are you talking about?"

"His nickname is Dragon. And her name is Megan."

Banks knew exactly who she was talking about now. "They've never been formally charged with anything." Banks finally spoke.

"Because you saw to it! Money can do a lot of things can't it? Except save you now."

"What am I being arrested for?"

"The kidnapping and endangerment of a child over a decade ago."

"You mean this nigga right here?" He said pointing at him.

"There is no statute of limitations on kidnapping." She looked behind her and said, "Take him away."

An hour later Banks was stripped and placed into a female holding cell. When he was processed and placed through the system, he carried his mattress, blankets, and personal items as he

By T. Styles

walked down the halls toward what would be his home.

Women from all around jaws dropped at how handsome the salt and pepper billionaire was who was entering the jail. Originally, they thought it was a mistake but after some time it became clear.

They had hit the jackpot just being in his presence.

When the door to his cell slammed shut, everything loving he felt for his son, Ace, vanished. He managed to stay out of situations like this all his life and now here he was, outwitted and outsmarted by his own hateful child.

Mason was right.

He underestimated Ace greatly, but it would never happen again.

Lying face up on the bunk, he thought about his plans. Surprisingly enough, since he could do nothing about anything, he had time to think.

And think he did.

In the end he would get his revenge.

Of this he was certain.

CHAPTER TWENTY-TWO
WALID
"Where is father?"

After Mason, Joey, Spacey and Walid entered Banks' home, they were irritated to see Ace propped up at Banks' desk. And after five minutes, to them, Ace had yet to say anything of value.

"Pops, do you remember the Greek story you told me of Icarus?"

Silence.

"I'll take your lack of answering as a yes." He laughed once and rose, while standing next to the window which lit up in shades of light blue off dark purple every time thunder clapped the sky. "In the story you told me about the boy who flew too close to the sun due to flying with wings made of wax."

"Get to your point."

"Well, your story has a flaw."

"Y'all feeling this nigga?" Spacey said, wondering why he hadn't been knocked on the head and bagged already.

"Chill," Joey whispered.

By T. Styles

"Had Daedalus, Icarus' father, not made trash wings, they both would have survived. And the sun would not have liquified the wings."

"You sound dumb, son. Where is Banks?"

"But you're right about comparing me with Icarus though." He pointed at him, refusing to stop his frame of thought. "Except it wasn't my fault things got as bad as they are right now in our family, as everybody likes to put on. And it wasn't Icarus' fault they both died either. Just like with my life, everything that I fucking am and do is because of father. He's the villain not me."

"Once again you speak about things you don't know." Mason responded. "I never told you they both died, son."

Ace blinked.

"Just Icarus. And if you aren't careful, even though you carry my blood in your veins, you will too."

"Is that a threat?"

"Do you want it to be?" Spacey pleaded.

Ace giggled.

"Where is father?" Walid pressed a bit harder.

"Before I tell you where he is, let me give you my stance on everything. You're going to have your opinions anyway but at least you'll hear where I'm coming from."

"Nobody cares." Joey said, clapping with each word.

"You see that's the problem." He beat his chest once. "It was always Walid!" He pointed at him. "Always everybody else. Nobody ever gave a fuck about me." He paused when he felt himself getting too emotional. Lowering his head, he took a deep breath and looked at each of them. "You better learn to try to understand me. Because I will tear the rest of Wales and Lou legacy down, I swear to God."

Mason, Spacey and Joey sighed.

"These are the things that led to father's demise..." Ace continued.

Mason's heart rocked.

And everyone looked at one another in complete fear.

"Are you saying that he's dead?" Mason felt dizzy.

He laughed, sat in the chair, and slammed his feet back on the desk. "Once upon a time..."

"One of these days you're going to regret all of this." Mason interrupted. "And you'll wish you could take it back but it will be too late."

Suddenly Mason's phone rang. Removing it from his pocket he glanced down and quickly answered. "Who is this?"

"You have a collect call from, *Banks*, from the women's correctional prison. To accept press one, to... "He rapidly accepted without allowing the message to continue.

Walking away from the group he learned quickly that his dearest friend was arrested and placed in a female jail. He was devastated for him and his heart broke at what this could do to his image but more than anything his peace of mind.

"I'm sorry this happened to you." Mason said passionately as he glared at Ace. "But know this, I'll be on top of it every night until you're brought home."

"I don't doubt it one bit, friend. What Ace has done is unrepairable. He's finally free."

"I got you for life."

When he ended the call, he walked back over to Ace. "You had him arrested?"

"Wait, what?!" Joey yelled.

"Why would you do that?" Mason said to Ace, his voice barely above a whisper.

"He should have left me alone. Y'all can be mad all you want but this is on him not me." He pointed at himself.

Spacey wanted to throw up.

And Walid walked up to a wall and slid down in shame.

"Is he in a female prison?" Joey questioned.

"No, stupid. Why would they put him in a women's prison?" Ace said.

It was at that time that they realized that either he was dumb or he really blocked out the past to save his account of the future.

"I'm going to see if I can get him." He looked at Ace. "You wanted out? Your wish is officially granted!" Mason rushed out without another word.

Slowly Walid rose and removed his jacket. Then he cracked his knuckles.

Spacey, and Joey stepped back to allow him to do what he must.

Realizing what was about to happen Ace stepped from behind the desk and approached him. He also removed his jacket.

Ace advanced closer.

Immediately Walid hit him with a blow to the right jaw followed by another to the left.

By T. Styles

Ace was dizzy for a moment but he quickly regained his bearings before striking him in the gut.

A gust of air released from his lungs and Walid hit him in the face again. He was trying to knock his head off his shoulders. Instead, he knocked him back towards his father's desk.

Papers floated to the floor.

But Ace was quick and charged him like a bull, by lowering his body. Under the weight, Walid fell flat on his back. A blow so hard that more wind flew from his chest causing him severe trouble breathing.

Spacey, wanting to get tagged in, was about to help when Walid yelled, "Stay out of it!"

Joey looked at Spacey and shook his head.

He had been wanting to get his hands on that boy's neck since he was a kid.

After a minute, Walid was able to get from up under Ace's wild jabs. Blow after blow ensued until both brothers were so bloody it was difficult to see their faces. Had it not been for Ace's wild hair, and their clothing choices, you could not tell one from the other.

At some point in the brawl Walid snapped.

His next ten blows were so hard and so consistent that Ace lost consciousness. Only then did Spacey and Joey pull him off.

Out of breath, Walid wobbled a bit but remained on his feet as the victor.

"That's for Aliyah. That's for Joey...and that's for father too." He said pointing down at him.

"You ain't say me," Spacey responded.

With nothing left to be said or done they all looked at Ace once more and walked out.

By T. Styles

CHAPTER TWENTY-THREE
ACE
"I might as well make things worse."

Sitting in the bedroom in his new penthouse Ace was in more pain than he let on.

Not only was the damage done to his body and face as a direct result of fighting with the one person he loved unconditionally in the world, but he started to have regrets for the move he made against his father.

He truly didn't comprehend how both Banks and Mason were his parents. And at the same time, he now understood that having him arrested was not only a blow to Banks' freedom but also his identity as a man.

Lying in bed, Arbella nursed the bruises on his face with extreme care. "You don't have to do so much."

"Ace, what are you talking about now?"

"I'm just saying I'll survive."

"I know you'll survive. You always do."

"You sound down."

"I'm your girl and you're hurt. Why wouldn't I be upset?"

"Thought you were my fiancé?"

"Maybe we should hold off on all of that right now. Focus on getting you better."

"You sound different. I wonder why." He moaned a little when she pressed down on an open scar. "Is it because I'm a loser?"

"Why did this happen?"

"I told you I don't want to talk about it."

"I just don't understand why your brother would do this to you. He seemed to care about you so much that it seems out of character."

"So you fucked him one time and now you're an expert?"

"Ace."

"I'm sorry." He paused. "But back in the day I may not have thought anything about you making a comment about Walid. But since I know you slept with him; do you really want to defend his good name?"

"Can you stop deflecting and tell me what happened?"

He took a deep breath.

To be honest, talking about it was the last thing he wanted to do. And at the same time, he realized how important it was for her that she knew a little because he could feel her pulling away.

206   By T. Styles

"I did something that I felt I had to do. For us to have our peace."

"What does that mean?"

"If I didn't make a move against my father, he would always come around. This time, I'm sure, he has left me alone forever."

"That's it?"

"That's all."

She sighed deeply. "Okay, whatever Ace."

"Why don't you go and get me something to drink."

"Water?"

"No, I mean something a bit stronger." She placed the soiled bloody gauze in the trash.

"Is that your way of getting me out of the house?"

Silence.

She sighed again. "Understood."

Before she left he said, "Arbella, I know you're confused right now. And I don't want this to come in between us. But do me a favor and stay the fuck out of my family business. Okay?"

She nodded. "I'll be back."

Now that he was alone with himself and his thoughts, he reflected on what changed. Throughout his life he wanted to get from up under

Banks' hold. At the risk of everything else. But it wasn't until that moment that he saw that not having him rule over all aspects of his life also put a wedge in the relationship with his brothers.

With Mason too.

And at the same time, he wasn't certain that he would have done things differently because in his mind he was so desperate to be free.

"Blakeslee!" He called out.

Silence.

"Blakeslee!"

After yelling a few more times to the point of his head hurting, she dipped into the room and jumped on the bed. The bounce hurt his temples which were throbbing at the moment.

"I need a Tylenol."

"Here you go." She had them in her hand and because they were warm, the uncoated pills were somewhat soggy.

He took them anyway with water on his nightstand. "Why did you have these in your hand so long?"

"'Cause I figured you'd want them. Was going to bring them to you earlier but Arbella was in the way. Where is she anyway?"

"She went out to get me something to drink." He paused. "Where have you been hiding though?"

"Not hiding, silly. Just spending time with him."

"Who? That little nigga you like?"

She laughed. "Even though you're being mean I'm going to give you a pass because at least you let me talk to him when father wouldn't."

"I told you I would."

"I don't understand why father or my other brothers are so overbearing. I keep telling them I'm not young acting like most girls my age. All the boys say it."

"Because they like to control everything."

"I know! And I hate that! Because you can't make people live by every rule you create. You have to give people freedom to find out who they are. But father's a tyrant who can't be reasoned with."

He looked at her and smirked. "How come you out here trying to sound all extra intelligent and shit?"

"It's because of him! My new boyfriend. He's so smart that he teaches me things I never even thought about before. Like he *showed me how to...*"

As she continued to talk his mind drifted away.

She went into detail about some things he should've paid extreme attention to.

Instead, his heart was tormented.

Because he was starting to feel utmost guilt for his actions against his family.

"So then he'll be able to..."

"I have to tell you something." He spoke, interrupting her rant.

"Okay you cut me off but what is it?"

"Father is locked up."

She sat up straight in his bed. "For what?"

"He did something when I was younger and now he has to pay for it."

She looked at her blood red nails and back at him. "But uh, is he going to be okay?"

"You know he always manages to come out on top."

She was concerned. "But how did they find out that he did something wrong back in the day?"

Hearing how scared she sounded had him fearing being too honest about his part in it all. He couldn't lose her too. So he said, "What's done in the dark always comes into the light."

"Does anybody else know?"

"The brothers, Minnesota, pops and Arbella."

By T. Styles

She lied back down. "Oh..." Staring at him as she lay on her side and he on his back she said, "You told Arbella first? Before me?"

"She's my fiancé."

"Well you know I don't like her right?"

"What you talking about? It was because of you that we got together. Don't you remember? When shit first went down you gave her my address."

"That's because I didn't want you to be alone. But I don't like her for you anymore. Besides, I'm here now. I'll take care of you."

"You want to tell me what's really going on or are you going to make me drag it out of you?"

"She does a lot of whispering when you aren't here and it makes me uncomfortable." She lied. "I mean, can you honestly say you trust her?"

He couldn't.

"It's just me but if I were you I would watch her."

"Why you telling me this?"

"Why wouldn't I tell you? She did fuck Walid. She may be fucking him again."

"Blakeslee. The language."

"Like I said, I'm starting to think she's not the girl for you."

"You talk to one boy on the phone and you become an expert in relationships? You still a kid."

She glared. "I'm actually only a few years younger than you."

"The key word here is *younger*."

"You're going to do what you want too so–"

"It's not about doing what I want, I'm just saying that you may be looking into things the wrong way."

"Maybe you're right. I mean, who would choose Walid over you?"

Everybody. He thought.

"So what you going to do about father? And our brothers?"

"Well everyone's mad at me so I might as well make things worse."

"Why?"

"Because it makes me feel better."

She laughed and kissed him on the side of his cheek and it stung. "Doesn't seem like you're better to me. All I see is sadness in your eyes. So...I have to leave." She sat up and scooted toward the edge of the bed. "Because your sadness makes me sad too." She hopped out.

When she was gone he thought about what she said.

By T. Styles

Was there more to Arbella that he didn't know?

Was she seeing Walid behind his back?

He had intentions on finding out.

CHAPTER TWENTY-FOUR
WALID
"Look at everything I've given you!"

Joey and Walid were in Urgent Care.

Walid was getting his hand stitched up while Joey sat in the waiting room dazed and confused. He was staring out into space but Walid knew what was on his mind.

His wife Sydney.

And what occurred with Ace and father.

When he was done he walked out to greet him. "Ready?"

He looked up at him. "Sit with me for a second."

Walid frowned and glanced around. "In here?"

Joey looked down. "Please, man."

Walid sat next to him.

"It doesn't look good for him getting out of jail."

Walid's stomach churned. "What you mean? I thought pops went to get him out."

"They trying to charge him with parental kidnapping. It's possible he could do five to ten years."

Just thinking about all of this being due to Ace drove Walid insane with rage. "So even though

214   By T. Styles

that's his son they can still lock him up for that old shit?"

Joey dragged a hand down his face and sat back in his chair. Arms crossed tightly over his chest. "They been wanting pops for as long as I can remember. Part of me thinks they're jealous about his success. The other part thinks they just angry that whenever something comes up regarding Mason or any of us, he's able to put money on the situation and make it go away."

"Like in Belize." Walid pulled breath into his lungs and released. "So what does that mean for the family?"

Joey looked at him and took a deep breath. "Even when he was gone, due to memory loss, for that period when he was Blaire..."

Walid squinted.

"It was when the three of you lived with his grandmother. I never felt we would lose him until now. And it got me feeling uneasy."

Walid nodded. "Me too."

"I'm just hoping he finds a way, because had he been on his game, he would not have been caught slipping."

"You think he can?"

"I need him to. We need him home."

Walid met Spacey at the hangar.

He was testing some controls and making sure his plane would be able to take flight with no problems, as well as the normal protocols that pilots had to go through when flying over America and internationally.

When Spacey saw him enter his plane he was surprised. "What you doing here, man? We not leaving until tomorrow."

Walid flopped in the co-pilot's seat. "I'm not going."

From the pilot's chair he swiveled his body and gave him his undivided. "Going where?"

"Back to the island."

"What you talking about? We're flying out tomorrow. It's what you wanted. So why is that changing now?"

He looked at him sideways. "You know why."

"Because of pops? Being locked up?"

"Yes!"

By T. Styles

Spacey placed a heavy hand on his shoulder. "This is the first time that I can remember that pops has ever been arrested. And if I allowed myself to think too much about it, I would probably react just like you. But what I know to be true is this...he always, *always* finds a way."

"But Joey thinks he–."

"Joey getting old." Spacey waved the air. "And everybody else getting old too if they think he won't come out on top." He paused. "Listen, pops will get himself out of this situation. He is literally the most brilliant man I know. A mastermind." He pointed at Walid's head. "And that brilliance that seeps through his blood lives in you too." He took a deep breath. "And Ace."

"I know...that's how he got hemmed up. He underestimated him."

"But Ace ain't smarter. He too selfish. Outside of his bitch he ain't got shit to fight for." He placed a fist over his heart. "But we do. We have each other. We have our family."

He nodded in agreement.

"All that little nigga did was back himself in a corner he won't be able to get out of." Spacey continued. "Shit will work out for pops though. We just gotta wait on the *when*."

"I don't doubt that he will but–"

"Don't miss your opportunity to save yourself, your girl and son. Your older brothers and Mason are here. And we're not leaving until we bring him home." He sat back. "If you don't want to go, base it off of your mind, not your heart."

"I hear you."

"We flying out tomorrow. I don't care what you say." He busied himself with the controls again. "As far as I'm concerned, something worse than this would have to happen for me to change my mind."

When Walid walked through the door he saw Aliyah standing in the center of the floor with his son in her arms and a suitcase packed.

Confused, he closed the door behind him. "We aren't leaving until tomorrow. Why you got your bags?"

"Walid..." she placed the sleeping baby in his crib next to the bed.

By T. Styles

When he saw her eyes were bloodshot red once again, he paused. "Wait what's going on? Is Baltimore okay?"

"Did you...did you kill my father?"

The room felt as if it were spinning. Out of all the hate Ace spewed, he reached back to spew more on his twin. "Aliyah..."

"Did you kill him?" He could tell that she was barely standing, she was in so much emotional pain. And he wanted to hold her but he was afraid he would fold too. "Walid...did you...did you kill my daddy?" She placed a hand over her heart.

"Baby, please don't do this."

"Answer the question!"

He gave her the entire story.

About how Ace got into trouble on the nearby island of Marjoca, a small town in Belize. And how he knew, per usual, that he would have to bail him out. And how when he found Ace being chased by a mob, he scooped him up in his truck. And it was that vehicle that accidentally slammed into her father, which caused injuries that later took his life. At several points in the story he wasn't sure if she heard a word he said she was crying so hard.

"I was working for your family during that time." She shook her head. "And you consoled me when I got the news, all while knowing that you were responsible. That's snake shit."

"Aliyah, I didn't want to hurt you. I didn't want you to look at me as the man who killed your father."

"Funny...because that's the only thing I can do right now."

"Baby, I was–."

"All you had to do was tell me the truth. All you had to do was be honest with me."

"I wanted to."

"Wanting to and doing it are two different things."

"You were distraught when you found out he was dead. I wanted to be there for you. And I figured if you knew it was because of me then you wouldn't let me help. And so I–"

"You chose to conceal the truth."

"Look at the life we have," he stepped closer. "Look at everything I've given you!"

"I don't care about materialistic things! I cared about you being honest. And now I'm realizing it's one thing after another with you and this family."

"Aliyah, we can work through this."

"How? Tell me how I can ever trust you again?" She placed a hand over her heart.

By T. Styles

"We have a son."

"And none of that matters."

"So...so...you gonna leave me behind this shit?"

Silence.

"If you walk out on me, I don't know how I'll react. I don't know what I'll do. I have spent the last couple of years of my life loving you. And loving our son. Yes, I concealed the truth, but you know my heart." He placed a hand on his chest.

"Do I?"

He rushed up to her. "Yes. Because if I'm certain about anything it's that I will never lie to you again. That I will always be honest with you."

"Except, when you think it'll protect me. Because that's what we're talking about isn't it?" She wiped tears away with a fist, reddening her eyes even more. "You think I'm too weak."

The fact that he was having to fight for his relationship as a result of his brother intensified the rage he felt against him in his heart. Ace was making it clear that if you weren't on his side you were a sworn enemy.

And Walid would never forget this shit.

Taking a deep breath, he stiffened up and spoke. "When did he tell you?"

"Does it matter?"

"You're going to leave me anyway." He shrugged hard. "You might as well tell me what I want to know. That's the least you can do."

"Today."

"Riddle me this...after all he did, why are you still accepting phone calls from this nigga?"

Silence.

He glared. "I'm waiting."

She laughed and walked over to their baby sleeping peacefully in his bed. "There's a saying I chose to forget from my father. He told me; *the worst thing you can do is idolize your heroes.* Yes, you saved me from poverty, and for that I will forever be grateful. But you are also untrustworthy. And it's that part of your character which gives me the strength to say it's over."

Walid felt gut punched.

"And I'm sorry." She continued.

Suddenly Walid stood stronger.

His body stiffened.

His head rose.

His heart hardened.

"You know...my fathers told me that you might not be the one." He pointed at her. "I couldn't see it then but it's apparent now. Because if you could look at me and think that I would do anything

By T. Styles

purposefully to hurt you, then it was over before it even began."

She looked down. "It's final."

"And to think, I almost gave you my fucking last name."

"Please don't."

"Where are you going?" He asked.

"Walid, I said it's over and–."

"This ain't about you no more, bitch! You got my fucking son!" He pointed at him.

Her eyes widened in fear. He had never gone on her so abrasively. "I...I mean...Sydney says I can stay with her. For now, that's my only option."

He stepped closer. "I'll allow that."

She trembled.

"But this is how it's going down. If I call for my son, you answer. If I want to see my son, you make it happen. If ever there is an issue, where I even think you trying to take Baltimore from me, I will take him from you, and you will never see him again. Are we clear?"

"Walid, I–."

"ARE WE CLEAR?"

"Ye...yes."

"Good, now get the fuck up out my house."

Crying, she grabbed Baltimore and her suitcase before rushing out the door.

By T. Styles

CHAPTER TWENTY-FIVE
BANKS
"Are you sure about that?"

The only positive thing was that the courtroom was virtually empty with the exception of Mason, Spacey, Walid and Joey who were waiting to take him home on bail, if all went in his favor. Despite the circumstances, he still looked good and they were grateful.

"All rise, for the honorable Peggy Wise."

Everyone rose.

And the judge, a middle-aged black woman with her hair pulled up in a tight bun, stepped behind the pod. "You may be seated."

Everyone sat down.

Banks stood next to his attorney for the bail hearing having all the confidence in the world that he would be released. So much so that he packed his bunk and items back in his cell.

"You may proceed." She said to the attorney.

"Your honor, I realize that you bear witness to many people speaking good things about their clients. But in my case what I'm prepared to share with you today is all true."

"I'm listening, counselor."

"My client has done more for the community than any person I know."

The judge laughed once. "Well, you must not know a lot of people. One of the things that being a judge affords me is the opportunity to see the charitable acts of many. And unfortunately for them all, they still stand before me having been accused of a crime."

"True. But my client is not a criminal."

"This is a bail hearing and I'm waiting on what you believe will help me make my decision to release him until trial. And I have to admit, so far I haven't heard anything but fluff."

"Okay, Mr. Wales donates one million dollars every year to The Children's Home For Wayward Boys in Baltimore city. He's also responsible for over 50 young men and women having gone to college. Most who are in their final stretches to become attorneys and computer scientists. Not only that, but he spends countless hours helping the community where he lived for over 14 years, while out of the country, by providing homes and jobs."

"And still he broke the law."

226   By T. Styles

"This bitch trying to throw pops away," Spacey said to his family.

"Nigga, you talking too fucking loud," Joey whispered in his face so hard Spacey's eyelashes fluttered due to the wind.

"Yes, Your Honor he did." The attorney proceeded. "He removed his son from the state's custody. But it was because he was concerned for his well-being and the lack of care he was given in that facility."

"The children's home is not on trial here."

"True, but my client was very concerned."

"It's funny. Because based on the records it appears that the child taken grew up to be the man who alerted us about the crime."

"Ace's snake ass." Spacey whispered.

Joey pinched him silent.

"His son is just angry, Your Honor. Family troubles." The attorney smiled, trying to make light.

"I've looked over this case. And as I recall there was a lot of damage to the city on the night the boy was taken from the home. Including the facility which was eventually blown up."

"Your Honor there is no evidence that my client was responsible."

"And there's no evidence that he wasn't either."

"Your Honor, he did not do that," Spacey yelled. "They trying to railroad my daddy!"

She glared. "Who are you?"

"Sit down!" Joey yelled, yanking him down. When he took his seat he asked, "Are you high?"

"Sorry, Your Honor," the attorney said. "That's my client's family."

"Well, they better learn to respect the rules of the courtroom, or I'll give them a crash lesson quickly."

Mason shook his head while Walid and Joey gave Spacey the *Care Bear Stare*.

"Sorry, Your Honor," Spacey said. "It won't happen again."

She nodded and focused on Banks and his attorney. "At the end of the day I'm quite possibly looking at the man who blew up the Children's Home, destroyed a few police cars and much more that night."

It was true.

She was looking directly at the nigga responsible.

"Your Honor, it seems like you've made up your mind."

"I have my opinions on this bail hearing but it's up to you to convince me otherwise. And I must admit, I haven't heard anything that will render me allowing bail or release on his own recognizance. You yourself said he has ties out of the country which makes him a flight risk."

"Your Honor, Mr. Wales is an amazing businessman. He isn't like the others you have in this prison. He's rich."

Banks wanted to pass out bearing witness to how bad his attorney was at the moment. He didn't have one in the states for criminal proceedings anymore because he had been out of the drug business for so long.

No worries.

He would have him replaced before the day's end that was certain.

She laughed. "Many of us aspire to being businessmen and women. I myself wanted to start a business that would provide legal services to people right on the scene with the click of a button. But it didn't happen like that. And even if it had it doesn't mean that if my child was in the state's custody, that I could bypass the law. So with that said I'm remanding him to our custody with no bail until trial."

"Your Honor, this isn't fair!"

"My decision is final."

———✈———

Banks was lying on his back, in his cell, thinking about his lack of success in court earlier in the day. It was the first time that he could remember where money couldn't buy him out of his predicament.

Frustration was building and he desperately tried to fight it because he understood from that point of view, it would be impossible for him to get out. The judge had made her decision so he would have to play by the rules.

For now anyway.

"Inmate number 52847."

Since it was Banks' number, he sat up and waited for the correctional officer. Before long, a slender female with an extreme smile on her face brought him a book with a letter on top of it. "I think this belongs to you, sir."

He knew the officer was sweet on him. She had told him how she loved his hair products, and how

By T. Styles

she followed his rise from Baltimore to Billionaire status.

But everyone knew she wanted to fuck.

Since he could benefit from all the graciousness in the world he winked. "Thank you, Zyla." He placed the items on his bed and sat back down.

"You're going to get out of here, sir." She said seriously.

Her confidence was heavy and he wanted more. "Think so?"

"I know so. I read up about you. I saw everything you've accomplished from being born in Baltimore and rising as high as you have in your businesses. How you always help others. I don't know what led you here but whatever I can do to help, know that I will. Even if it means losing my job."

He lowered his head. "Are you sure about that?"

She grabbed the bars and put her face through the slots. "If you want to get out of here tonight, say the word and I'll do it." She whispered seriously.

"Thank you, I'm good. But I may need to take you up on that later."

"Know that I'm ready when you are."

When she walked away he grabbed the letter and looked at its contents. It was from Minnesota.

Lying face up, he read every word.

Dear Dad,

I haven't been able to get a night's sleep since I realized you were in jail. I don't understand why Ace did what he did, and it's hard to comprehend.

So I won't try.

Although he's my brother and I want to love him, I'm having so much trouble. We may be many things but snitches and hurting each other is not the Wales Way. At the same time I remember when I made a mistake by mailing a letter which got Harris locked up many years ago.

Needless to say I'm confused.

Is he more like me than I want to believe?

LOL.

Anyway, I want you to remember what we talked about alone in your office. About your grandmother and what she did to me and Spacey.

I need you to look at this book.

I need you to <u>understand this book</u>.

And I need you to come up with another plan. Everybody has a weak spot and although revenge

By T. Styles

may not help get you out of prison, maybe it will
teach Ace a lesson he won't soon forget.

Put the letter down for a second and think about
what he wants more than anything...

Banks closed the letter momentarily and
thought hard about the question.

"The girl." He said to himself. "But what else?"

It took some time but he said, "Freedom."

He read the letter again.

When you are clear on what he wants, turn it on
his head. We will get you out of jail no matter what.
But Ace cannot get away with this shit.

I'm awake from my misery.

Which means I'm ready to serve this family in
blood.

Love,

Minnesota Wales.

Banks closed the letter and picked up the book.
It was titled *Brainwash Love by Gemma Holmes*.
For the next few days, he spent hours poring over
every detail about the book.

A few things materialized from his intense
focus.

For the first time ever, he realized how wicked his grandmother presented herself to his kids when he didn't know. The fact that his children experienced so much turmoil which was designed to break them down emotionally troubled him and had him looking at her differently in death.

Second, he witnessed how systematic the book presented steps to get a person to do whatever they wanted. At first he didn't understand why Minnesota gave him the book but after some time it became clear.

And he would use it to his advantage.

When he was able, he made several phone calls.

It was time to get his life back on track.

Mason and Spacey waited in the lobby of a skyrise building for what seemed like forever.

Spacey had flown them to Texas for a weekend trip on his jet and they were exhausted. But he understood what was required based on Banks'

By T. Styles

call and would do anything in his power to bring Banks home.

"I still can't believe he's locked up." Spacey spoke.

"Me either. I haven't allowed myself to go that deeply to be honest."

"He gotta be stopped." He looked to his left and then his right before leaning closer to Mason. Whispering, he said, "Something happened yesterday while Walid was driving that made me feel like a hit was placed on his head."

"What you talking about?"

"Someone shot in front of the car he was driving out Baltimore. I put it off like he may have gotten mixed in a possible drive by, but I don't know. I mean, you think Ace would go this far?"

Mason breathed deeply. "The thing is this...at one point, you wanted to kill me, I wanted to kill Banks and we all wanted to kill each other."

"True," Spacey said, remembering the good old days.

"But we all had somebody on our left or right, that brought us back to our senses. Made us realize how important we are to one another. Ace ain't got that. He's disconnected. And worse than it all, he's isolated. What's the best way to deal with people who reject you?"

"He's gonna kill our asses."

"Exactly."

Spacey shook his head and sat back. "I never liked him."

"I realize that."

"I'm serious. I remember having conversations with him trying to get him to stay on track but he was always on some weird shit."

Mason took a deep breath. "What's about to happen to Ace will be the most difficult thing we've ever had to deal with in terms of a war. The enemy is literally in our family this time, of me and Banks' bloodlines. But I don't want you to base your relationship with your brother off our actions, whatever they may be."

He waved the air. "Nah, you better go to Joey and 'em with all that shit. He been drew the line with me."

"Ms. Armstrong will see you now." A secretary stepped up to them. "Right this way."

As they followed her down the corridor Mason took a deep breath.

He only hoped Banks' plan would be solid enough to work.

236   By T. Styles

CHAPTER TWENTY-SIX
SIX MONTHS LATER
ACE

"I'm not like father. I will hurt you."

For the past two months Ace's world seemed to be coming down around him.

First with the exception of Blakeslee, no member of his family wanted to have anything to do with him.

He called Walid...nothing.

He called Mason and he didn't answer the phone.

He called Spacey and he told him to suck his dick.

He even called Minnesota and she said, "You dead to me."

Out of desperation, he tried to plant Blakeslee by having her call their family. They told her virtually the same thing. "You picked a side, now stay there."

For the first time ever he felt the pang of not having family. He never stopped to realize that the power he felt in life, prior to having his father arrested, came from a result of being a Wales.

THE GODS OF EVERYTHING ELSE 2   237

Without the prestige, he felt like nothing.

He was on his way back from the bank when he tried to reach Arbella. She had always been distant, but over the past few months it had gotten worse. He knew he had to speak to her so he couldn't drive home fast enough to talk.

No more games.

She would either tell him what was happening and why she had gone missing, or he would beat it out of her.

Dropping his keys on the end table next to the door he rushed toward his bedroom. "Arbella!"

She didn't answer.

So he assumed she once again wasn't home.

He would have gotten her whereabouts from the application, but it recently became obvious that she removed the tracker which left him clueless at the moment.

Exiting his room, and hoping for answers, he went to Blakeslee's room instead. The moment he knocked on the door she shoved herself out and slammed it closed behind her.

Her hair was messy and as usual she wore so much makeup she looked trashy. Something was off.

He frowned. "Have you seen Arbella?"

By T. Styles

"No." She wiped her mouth and then cleared her throat. "You know I don't get along with that bitch."

"Why you acting crazy?"

"I'm not acting crazy, silly. I was only answering your question."

He looked over her shoulder at the closed-door. "Do you have company?"

"Yes. I told you I was going to have company today. Remember? We were talking about father getting locked up in your bed. It was right after the fight you had with Walid. I told you he would be in town today and you said okay."

It was during the time when Ace blacked out while she was talking. After Banks was arrested. Even if he said yes, he reserved the right to change his mind. And so, he shoved his way into her bedroom.

Lying on the bed was a thirty-two-year-old man with more gray hair than Banks. It wasn't the kid she had shown him in the past.

"What the fuck?" He yelled. "How...how old are you?"

He stood on his knees and said, "I told her I wanted to meet you, but we're in love."

Ace was heated because his dick was glossy with his little sister's juices and the scent of sex in the air caused his stomach to churn.

Looking at Blakeslee although everything was obvious, he said, "Hold up, are you sleeping with this grown ass man?"

Before she could respond he took his fist and pounded the stranger in the center of his face. The blows were repetitive until his nose was literally as soft as mashed potatoes.

Blakeslee clawed at Ace's shoulders and back, drawing blood each time, but Ace didn't feel the pain.

It was useless.

In the end, Ace had successfully taken out all his rage on the older man. But the true reasons for the brutal beating were more complicated.

He was mad at Arbella and her distance.

He was mad about his family leaving him alone which was a classic case of be careful what you wish for.

And he was now mad that his little sister had taken advantage of the freedom he provided by sleeping with a grown man.

After whipping him senseless, he tossed him out naked, with nothing to wear but his shoes and shirt.

When the door slammed, he grabbed her by the arm and flung her on the sofa. "Fuck is wrong with you? Huh?"

She hiccupped. "You said you would never do that." She wept. "You said you would let me have my freedom and now I see you're just like father. You're just like all men."

"Say what you want but I will not allow you to be a whore in my crib." Standing tall he said, "You are not to leave this house, Blakeslee! And you better listen to me too! I'm not like father. I will hurt you."

He stormed out.

CHAPTER TWENTY-SEVEN
BANKS

"Anyone for my plan, raise your hand."

W alid, Mason, Joey, Spacey, Minnesota and Faye all stood in court while Banks posted up before the judge. Banks made a serious move by waiving his right to a jury trial.

The family wasn't feeling the shit.

But Banks, with Mason's help, did it anyway. Because if all went as planned, it would cause him to be a free man by trusting the judge fully.

After the prosecution, and Banks' new dynamic young black female attorney submitted their cases, the judge who was not a fan gave her verdict.

She alone held Banks' life in her hands.

We're talking about a possible ten-year sentence here.

"I have heard both sides of the case. And after taking a lot of time to go over the details and what Mr. Wales intended to do in an effort to save his son, the State of Maryland is dropping all charges."

The Wales clan exhaled in relief.

Banks and Mason smiled.

She beat her gavel to silence them before returning to the verdict.

In the end she stated that she believed that Banks' although irresponsible, had Ace's best interest at heart. And that she didn't see any further reason to give him a harsher sentence.

After dismissing the court, Banks rushed up and embraced his family in the courtroom. Due to the excitement, the bailiff escorted them *that way*, which resulted in the celebrations taking place in the lobby.

Focusing on Mason first, Banks said, "Thank you for handling this. I would not be free without you."

He smiled. "As many times as you've saved me?" He wiped the air with his hand. "I figured it was my time to step up and I'm glad I could do that for you. Besides..." He looked at Faye. "She was the one who came through in a clutch. She could've gotten arrested but she didn't care."

Banks nodded. "Thanks again, friend. I will never forget this shit."

He walked over to her and she was as stunning as usual. Every curve of her body introduced itself to his eyes. "I realize asking you to do what you did was heavy."

"You mean bribing a judge with an app?" She whispered.

He smiled.

"It was, but it was also a long shot." She explained. "But when I met with her and shared with her my ideas for her legal app she was overly excited. I could tell she had a passion for helping people pulled over by the police that extended past her robe."

"Wow."

"I allowed her to see my references and my resume, and she learned that what I normally charge was way more than a judge earns in a year."

"So you got her excited first before you dropped the price." Mason added.

"Yes. She was so disappointed that her dream wouldn't happen due to not being able to afford my fee, until I mentioned a friend that needed a little help in jail. And that if she helped me, I'd help her."

"She wanted it enough to risk it all?" Walid asked.

"There's nothing more powerful than having a dream only to have the possibility of that dream be taken away. So yes. She definitely went for it."

Banks picked up on the judge's desire at his bail hearing. Luckily, he remembered it for later.

He was brilliant per usual.

"Can I talk to you in private?" He asked.

She nodded and they stepped further away from the family. "So...so you know about me?"

"What you mean?"

"That I...you know...was born a..."

"Yeah, and I don't care."

He exhaled. "I'm about to enter a busy period in my life, but if you would allow me, I'd love to get to know you better."

"What do you think I put my job on the line for? I'm literally waiting on you." She kissed his cheek and walked away.

Minnesota wore a huge smile on her face. Spacey, Joey and Walid clowned him in the lobby while Mason nodded his head.

Walking back up to them he said, "We have to tend to family business now."

Mason sighed. "I heard about the guards you hired before you got arrested. The ones who watched the kids. Why did you destroy their homes, Banks?"

"Because I said I would."

"But you had their homes burned down. Their families were displaced."

"The old Banks has returned. From here on out if I make a threat, I'm following through." He pointed at the floor. "And had they been on duty, Blakeslee would've never left with Ace. Especially the nigga on her detail." He paused. "You should understand. If you ask me, I'm waiting on the old Mason to return too."

Mason looked at him square on. "Do you really want that shit?"

Spacey, Joey, Minnesota and Banks looked at one another remembering how wicked he could get and chose to remain quiet. Besides, Ace was enough trouble for them all.

"Did you give that money to Zyla?" Banks continued. "She treated me good in jail. Let me make extra calls, sent messages out and everything."

"The correctional officer?" Mason asked.

He nodded.

"We had one hundred thousand delivered in cash per your request." He chuckled once. "She quit her job while we were standing in front of her."

Banks laughed and got serious. "We need to go home and meet in the lounge. What I'm about to tell you most of you won't like. But it's necessary all the same."

246   By T. Styles

The family looked at one another not knowing that the worst was yet to come.

They were all dressed in black in the lounge at Banks' home. The Triad was sent away with more experienced security guards who were former secret service agents to protect them.

So Banks could speak to his family in private without worrying about their safety.

After hearing what he learned, the family was beyond disappointed at Ace.

Again.

They all knew that there was a possibility that Ace could be a monster but this was taking it to a different level.

"He was going to have me killed?" Walid said, mostly to himself. "Over a girl?"

"I told you," Spacey said to Mason, referring to the fake drive-by.

"Yes. Recruited one of Valentine's men." Banks continued. He knew this tore his son up, but it was important for him to have all the details. "And I'm sorry, Walid."

"But why would he do that? We had our beef but...death?"

"Because he's a selfish ass nigga." Spacey explained. "This is why I never liked or trusted him. I mean have we really forgotten the fact that he pushed Celeste down the stairs as a child? Which fractured her skull and to this day put her in a wheelchair where she will never speak or move again?"

Most had forgotten that he exhibited forms of extreme rage as a child. Because most wanted to act as if it didn't exist.

But Spacey didn't.

"So what are you going to do?" Walid asked. "Because he took everything from me. My girl...and even the island." He looked at Minnesota, Spacey, Joey, Mason, and Banks. "I'm not going to let him take y'all away too."

"You said it brother," Spacey added.

"And then there's the murder Walid was involved in that needs our sincerest attention."

"Murder?" Mason said, with raised eyebrows.

"What you talking about?" Spacey said.

"Back home, when the old man was run over and eventually killed, Walid was actually behind the wheel, not Ace. And he's threatening him. In the past I wouldn't think Ace would go rat but look what just happened to me."

Spacey was livid. "This nigga really out here loving on the police? Do he know we got secrets? He gotta go now!"

"That's why I wanted to bring you all here. Because you may not understand my next move. But I want us to make this decision as a family. But if anybody votes against it, any of you at all, I will go the other way. But you must vote all the same."

Banks explained his plan and when he was done he took the vote.

They couldn't believe what they had heard.

"Anyone for my plan, raise your hand."

Spacey raised his hand so fast, he almost busted Minnesota in the face who was sitting next to him.

Joey was second.

Minnesota was next.

It took a moment but Mason followed.

Everyone focused on Walid. After five minutes, and they allowed him the time, he raised his hand too.

Banks took a deep breath.

"So what now?" Mason asked.

"The first part of my plan I already put into action while in jail. That's why Zyla was instrumental because she got my messages through."

"What that mean?"

"It involved Arbella and her father. Let's just say that the nigga Valentine loves me."

They laughed.

"The final part of the plan I'm putting into action now."

By T. Styles

CHAPTER TWENTY-EIGHT
ACE
"All I care about is you."

When Ace returned to the penthouse he saw Blakeslee was gone...

Word on the street she returned home.

He wasn't to upset because he believed that he would have to hold her up emotionally, after she realized how painful it would be to seriously be without the family. So her absence, in a way, gave him some relief.

But where was his girl?

In the past she came home and they would move awkwardly around the penthouse in an effort to stay out of each other's way. But last night she didn't bother to come back.

He even bit the bullet and called Mr. Valentine, who had always made himself available.

He didn't answer either.

Sitting on the sofa, with his world crashing down around him he was shocked when she called from a number he didn't recognize. "Where are you?"

"I want to speak to you in person. Can you meet me?"

"I don't trust you so we'll meet somewhere of my choosing."

"Whatever you want."

"If you take more than five minutes to get there then stay wherever the fuck you are."

Eight minutes later they met at a pool which was closed for the season. He could tell that her eyes were different and that something was off. Had he paid more attention to her in the past, instead of setting up botched hits for his family members, he would have seen this wasn't a new change.

But just like everything else, he had dropped the ball.

Standing in front of her he said, "What took you so long?"

"It was only three minutes. And I had to do something right quick."

"What is this about, Arbella?" He looked around while standing in front of her, just to be sure it wasn't an ambush.

"I can't be with you right now. The way that you are."

"What does that mean?"

By T. Styles

"Over the past few months, my father has made me see that you don't really care about me. He's made me see that you don't really care about anybody."

"This man possibly burned your mother's body and your businesses to the ground, and I'm the one that you're in fear of?"

"My father believes that we should separate and put more space between us. Until you can grow up. I really want to be with you but not until my father believes it's the right time."

He threw his arms up. "Why do you keep bringing up your father?"

"My father believes that—"

"I just asked why you keep bringing up your father and you bring him up again?"

"You should really respect my father more, Ace. He believes that and I do too. My father also believes that you should respect your father more too. That if you did respect your father more we wouldn't be in the situation we're in right now."

Something was off.

She sounded brainwashed.

"Wait, who's speaking to me right now? You? Your father? Or mine?"

She blinked a few times and it was obvious that she wasn't fully understanding the question although she was desperately trying. "I have to go, Ace. I'm sorry."

He grabbed her hand softly. "Listen, I won't pressure you. But I want to leave you with something."

"My father is waiting and–."

"Arbella, please."

She nodded.

"I don't know how my father was able to get through to yours, but he has. The whole objective is to tear down my world. I'm sure Valentine gave him his price. But if he takes you away, he succeeded in taking the only thing I care about. I mean, I thought we were forever?"

She looked down and he could tell the struggle was hard. "I'm...I'm so confused."

"My head is fucked up right now, Arbella. And yours is too. I thought we could handle this shit but maybe we can't right now. Maybe we really are just kids. But you are the one for me. I feel it. I'm realizing that...maybe I shouldn't have tried to pull you from your father but at this point, I don't care about none of that shit. All I care about is you."

He received a text message that rocked his world.

She cried softly.

"I have to go. He was released today and there's a possibility that they'll be looking for me. But I want you to know that whatever this is that's happening to us, that I don't blame you. And at some point, you're going to come back to me." He placed a hand over her heart.

It pounded under his palm.

"Ace...I..."

"Please, come back to me. And when you do I'll be waiting."

He kissed her on the cheek and ran away.

After being weirded out by Arbella's new tune, Ace went to the ATM. Receiving the message that Banks was released scared him greatly. So he wanted to withdraw as much money as he could before requesting a cashier's check from the bank in the morning when they opened.

But after entering his code into the system he was faced with his worst fear.

All his money, every single cent, was gone.

He placed the code in a million times but after the 10th attempt, he finally understood.

He was broke.

Tossing the card across the parking lot, he slid down the wall.

Just then his phone rang.

With nothing left to do he answered. "Baby, baby are you there?"

It was Arbella and she sounded frantic.

"Yes. It's me."

"You're right...I...I think this attention that my father has been giving me lately was only to get back at you. I don't know why I didn't see it before but when I stood in front of you, all I wanted was to run away with you. Maybe we can do that now before–."

"You gave them the code to my bank, didn't you?"

Silence.

"Arbella...just tell the truth."

"No...but I overheard from my father a moment ago that Blakeslee did."

He sighed deeply. With the code all online transactions were possible. Including the transfer of the rest of his millions. "I'm glad it wasn't you."

Just then he saw a black Aston Martin pull up across the parking lot. When it parked both Mason and Banks stepped out.

By T. Styles

The sun hit both of them and they looked like they were superstars on the set of a video. Mason leaned against the side of the car while Banks approached his son.

He was wearing all black, smoked shades and a look of seriousness.

Arbella continued. "But they made me put a tracker on your car. That's why I was a few minutes late. You should–."

"I have to go, Arbella. I love you. And no matter what happens, I will come back to you. Unless I'm dead." He ended the call and dropped it next to him.

"Get up." Banks paused, as he tugged at the side of his glasses to make sure they were in place. "You're coming with me."

"So you about to kidnap me again?" He said looking up at him, as the sun shielded his view. "Didn't you just get home from doing shit like this?"

"You not a kid no more. This a straight up snatching, nigga. Now get the fuck up!"

CHAPTER TWENTY-NINE
WALID
"Without you, there's only one of me."

Walid, Banks, Mason, Minnesota, Joey and Spacey stood in front of Ace inside the lower floor of a building under construction.

Walid was directly in Ace's eyeline.

"Hey, brother," Ace said, attempting to find humor.

"My girl left me."

"Mine too." He chuckled once. "I guess we back in the world like we entered it. Alone and together."

Walid smiled once although he found nothing funny. "If someone told me five years ago I could look at you and hate you, I wouldn't believe them. But I get that shit now."

That hurt and Ace was on attack mode again. "It's so easy for y'all to make me the villain isn't it?" He looked at each of them.

"You did that to yourself. Since you was a kid." Spacey responded.

"I would expect your bitch ass to speak first. You never liked me. So now, in your opinion, everything you thought about me is true."

By T. Styles

"You broke code, son." Mason said. "And because you don't know the kind of family we are, you don't realize how devastating that is to your life."

Fear rose in his blood. "If y'all going to do whatever you want to do then do it. I don't even care anymore." He looked at Walid. "Even turned my own brother against me. I mean who does that shit? We twins!"

"We're not brothers." Walid said. "Without you, there's only one of me."

His heart pounded. "If that's the case then why you talking to me?"

"Because I wanted that to be the last thing I ever say to you." He walked up, spit at his feet and walked away.

Banks stepped up. "Anything else to say?"

"You want me to speak some shit that will make it easier to kill me? Well I ain't gonna do it!" He looked at all of them, sweat running down his face and dampening his hair. "Do you hear me? I ain't gonna do it."

"Fair enough." Banks said.

He looked behind him and Spacey grabbed a bag from his back pocket and slammed it over Ace's head all hard and shit.

The darkness choked the bravado from his chest.

A panic attack was approaching.

"So you can't even do it to my face?" Ace yelled from underneath the hood. "You need to place a bag over my head to do your dirty work? If you gonna kill me, look in my eyes! You hear me? Look in my eyes!"

"Nah, we good." Spacey said. "Seen enough of you."

Ace prepared himself for the sting of having a bullet rip through his body. Instead, he felt a prick in his arm before he passed out.

By T. Styles

EPILOGUE

When Ace opened his eyes, he was shocked to discover that he was lying in a ditch and that the sun was beaming down on his face.

He was getting scorched by the rays.

In fact, he was so sunburned, that his skin stung to the touch.

Believing he was on the verge of being buried alive, he quickly crawled halfway out of the ditch. A few feet to the left, he saw men packaging what looked to be cocaine.

"Oh, sleeping beauty is finally up," one Mexican man said with his three remaining teeth hanging on for dear life. His accent was thick and reminiscent of the country. He walked over to a bucket of water, scooped some out with a ladle and handed it to him. "Drink up."

The water was cloudy and contaminated, but he was so thirsty he would take the risk and downed every drop. "More."

The man did it again.

"More."

He did it once more.

"More!"

"Get the fuck out of the hole! You don't have servants here my friend." He wagged his finger in front of him.

Ace crawled all the way out. His body pressing on the hot dirt. "Where...where am I?"

"Mexico."

"Mexico...I don't...I don't understand."

"You don't need to understand. You need to work." He lowered his height. "Now get the fuck up and help us. We have a huge shipment that's going out tonight. And the boss doesn't like us to mess up the package."

"Who's the boss? Bring him to me at once!"

The man kicked him in his face, forcing blood to spew from his lips. Red splatters dampening the dirt. "The next thing I do will be final. Now get up before I put you in that hole forever!"

For the next few weeks, Ace spent his mornings packaging cocaine and his nights drinking tequila. He aged so much that it was difficult to believe that he was only nineteen years old.

No one cared who he was or about his past.

In fact, there were about fifty people around him with painful stories. So he could keep his tales of the rich billionaire son to himself.

At first, the busyness kept his thoughts at bay.

It wasn't until six months in that he experienced a mental breakdown. Up until that moment he held onto hope that Banks was teaching him a lesson. But after more time passed and his father hadn't shown his face, he realized something much darker was happening.

And that possibly, just maybe, Banks and the others were really done.

He later discovered that he was sold off for a dime.

Upon hearing the news, Ace made an escape. He looked like a madman, as a beard had taken over his face and his wild hair was matted and untamed.

Wearing only torn khaki pants, he was so dirty you could hardly see his tribal tattoos.

An hour later, barefoot, he ended up in a small town that was a mix of authentic Mexican life and a tourist trap. The roads were mostly unpaved and flooded with red dirt, but small quaint eateries were lined on each side of the block.

Out of breath and hungry, Ace located a payphone. Quickly he snatched the handset off the hook and then was overcome with a hard truth.

Not only did he forget everyone's contact information, relying on stored numbers in his cell back in the day, but he also didn't have identification or no way to get money if he reached anyone. Not to mention that every single person who would have flown to get him, he burned the bridge connecting them together.

And so he was officially alone.

When he smelled the food coming from a restaurant, he tried to enter to get a bite to eat. A worker shooed him away with the broom and Ace landed in front of a window where a newlywed couple was eating inside.

"Look at that man," the American man said.

"He looks so sad." The woman said.

"Don't feel sorry for him!" The man announced, pointing at her. "You can achieve anything you want in life. You just have to go for it."

"Should we give him something to eat?"

"Nope." He shrugged. "Today is about us. Plus I can smell him from here." He laughed. "Let him starve for all I care." He called the manager over and he quickly shooed Ace away.

Sitting by a trash can, with flies buzzing about, he cried. He was what they called in America, a hot ass mess. And it would only get worse. With nothing left to do he returned to the cocaine ranch, in total defeat and despair.

Later on that night, Ace was overcome with grief once again.

He was finally realizing that this was his new life.

The old life had vanished.

He could either perish or cry.

Months later, when a rich young Mexican woman who smelled of expensive perfume entered the bunk area where most of the workers slept, Ace was reminded of his old life. His time was so consumed with activity and hard work, that he forgot the past.

It was too painful to remember anyway.

Instead he met people from Mexico who had harsh upbringings and lifestyles he could have never imagined. He immersed himself into their stories and found himself being ashamed of his greed and the way he disrespected the locals in Belize.

Before long Ace Wales was gone and the name Cabello Salvaje took its place. Which meant *wild horse* in Spanish. He earned the moniker for his untamed hair.

In the end, Ace had officially been broken down.

When the woman moved closer with sandwiches and fresh water, Ace was ashamed of his condition. He smelled so badly he could hardly stomach his own odor. And yet, the woman didn't appear to care.

"Are you hungry?" She asked.

He nodded and shuddered at her kindness.

She handed him the food and he tore into it like a dog.

"Thank...thank you."

A few years ago, he ate meals shipped from the freshest waters and lands on earth...and now none of it mattered.

Suddenly, with a mouth full of bread Ace wept harder.

She placed the other sandwiches down and sat on the bunk next to him. "Are you okay?" She put a hand on his back.

"Please don't do that. I...I smell."

"I don't care. And if you knew where I came from you would understand why. Now please, tell me, what's wrong?"

Ace appreciated the attention but he didn't want to say who he was.

Although the people he worked with were nice, they were also unaware of his past billionaire status. This was on purpose. He didn't want anybody to try and make a come up by snatching

266

him and asking for ransom he was certain his father would not pay.

"It's just that I finally realized I ruined my life."

"Don't say that. If you want to rise high, Kordell will help you. You just have to prove yourself first."

"Kordell?"

"Yes. That's my husband. And that's who you work for. Didn't you know?"

He didn't.

"Listen, don't worry. Everything will be okay. I see power in your eyes. Use it."

Ace didn't know who Kordell was, but he was certain that he was more than likely a friend of his father's. And that maybe if he listened to her, he could rise high in the organization before returning to America.

And finding Arbella.

Maybe even making amends with Banks and Walid.

Later on that night he was asleep in the bunk thinking about the possibilities when a hand was suddenly slammed down on his face. Had they pressed any harder, they would've stolen the breath from his lungs.

Placed in the back of a van he was now looking into the eyes of another stranger.

Nicolas Rivera.

Banks' sworn enemy, who was supposed to be dead.

Unfortunately, Kordell made the mistake of thinking the shoot-out at the airport when he saved Banks, also took the life of the grimiest killer in Mexico's history.

He was wrong.

And so, the error allowed Banks' child to be taken under the cover of night.

"So, you are the son of the great Banks Wales?" He smelled horribly too.

"Who are you? And what do you want with me?"

"You can consider me a friend." He placed a hand over his heart. His nails were so soiled they looked like a black tipped French manicure. "I can't believe that Banks' son is really here. You are as pretty as a girl."

Ace remained silent.

"I mean when they told me about the Wild Horse, I had to see for myself. You didn't disappoint my friend."

"My father won't pay for me. If you take me, it will get you nothing."

"Oh...I don't want ransom."

He frowned. "Then what do you want? He doesn't care about me. That's why I'm here."

"I agree with you, friend." He placed a hand on his chest and nodded erratically. "I have always wanted a son myself. And now I have one."

"What does that mean?"

"I will teach you everything I know."

"And what do I have to give you in return?"

"You just have to love me. And let who I am, and what I represent, live through you." He placed a soiled hand over Ace's hardened heart.

Ace exhaled.

With a fly landing on his nose Nicolas said, "Nothing less. Nothing more."

TWO YEARS LATER

Banks never came back for Ace and Kordell continued to lie and say he was at the cocaine ranch during the few times he mentioned his son in passing.

And as a result, Ace was forced to be raised by a man so wicked, he couldn't believe some of the things he witnessed.

Murders.

Robberies.

Maiming.

Ransom.

And yet, despite it all, Nicolas' love for Ace was focused and intense. He kept his word by teaching him everything he knew. The trouble was the only thing he knew was how to kill and get revenge.

Because Banks wouldn't put Nicolas on, and tried to have him killed by Kordell, every day he told his son how he didn't love him and how his own father hated him and wished he had never been born. It was easy to believe it was the truth because Banks never tried to rescue him.

And so, Nicolas and Cabello spent months taking from others.

These horrendous acts, coupled with Ace's seething hate for his father was the main reason why, while standing over Nicolas' grave, he vowed to live up to all the man represented.

Nicolas was about that old school revenge.

The type that seeped in the spirit every day until it was ripe and ready to attack. This was that classic shit that took years to create.

And Banks, clueless of his existence, had no idea.

The funeral ceremony was small and had an undisclosed location. Besides, Nicolas had so many enemies that there were some who would rather dig up his bones and grind them to sand before allowing him to have a resting place.

But Ace had come to love the man.

He came to understand the man.

And now it was time to go home with the reputation the feared moniker known as Wild Horse had provided for him in Mexico.

First, to find the love of his life, Arbella Valentine.

Next, he wanted revenge on Banks.

Lastly, he wanted revenge on Walid.

Cabello Salvaje had intentions on getting everything due him no matter what.

THE WALES AND LOU'S

Banks had gotten married to Faye Armstrong on the beautiful Wales Island...

It was a small ceremony with Mason as his best man, and Spacey, Walid, The Triad and Joey as his groomsmen. Faye wanted Minnesota in her party. She said yes. Coupled with Faye's friends and family, the wedding was a spectacular event.

Banks Wales, the billionaire, was officially off the market.

Life had changed somewhat over the years.

Sydney had a child back in America which no one in the Wales family claimed. The theory was that even though the boy possessed Wales blood, due to him being Ace's son, his father had been outcast and that made him an outcast too.

But Sydney didn't care. She was a mother who was on cloud nine. The only thing the Wales' did was ensure that a monthly stipend came in the boy's name. He was called Roman Wales and as far as they were concerned, he would never be a part of the legacy.

272   By T. Styles

But Sydney wasn't the only one with a child.

Back on the island, Blakeslee now had a two-year-old little girl called Sugar Wales. The child was a direct result of the stranger who she slept with while living with Ace. But she was far from mother material. Instead, she was the whorish of all whores when it came to being promiscuous. The number of men she slept with was untold and most turned their head to her acts.

She had been stricken with so many venereal diseases she stank when she walked.

Luckily Minnesota always wanted to have a child. And so she stepped up and loved on her two-year-old niece as if she were her own.

Spacey helped and did a great job too.

Whenever Blakeslee felt guilty about not being a mother, she would promise to take the child away but was quickly threatened with every inch of her life by Banks. The deal was Minnesota got to keep the baby, and she got to keep her men, hoe lifestyle and stipend.

So for now, Blakeslee, now eighteen, backed away.

The only one that felt for her was Mason. She looked so much like Banks when he was younger that he was weakened around her. Recognizing this, she played on this power and so he kept his distance.

Spacey settled down with the girl who had always been in the picture and although he was far from making her his wife, he did tell her he was ready for them to be together. And that was all she needed to hear before moving into the house and living amongst the royal family.

Walid decided against love for the moment. He wasn't necessarily a playboy, but he was something like it. Whisking women from island to island. Showering them with gifts and diamonds. He was the thing billionaire romance stories were made of. Except, every time he would fall for a girl he would find an excuse to cut her off later.

But everyone knew where his heart truly lied.

He was and would always be in love with Aliyah.

But there's more!

Thanks to Spacey, Walid was an outstanding pilot. And once a month he would fly back to the States to see his son Baltimore. He loved the child wholeheartedly and at one time considered removing him from his mother to live on Wales Island. The thought was inspired by Banks and Mason feeling as if his life was in danger back at

By T. Styles

home. But Walid felt she was a good mother. He himself knew what it felt like not to have a mother's love. And so, he allowed the boy to live with her and Sydney back in America.

Joey told him several times that he didn't trust his ex-wife, Sydney.

He chose not to listen.

Was it a mistake?

Joey on the other hand got close to Mason. The two of them created an unlikely friendship that was built on the foundation of being single. At one point Mason did have a girlfriend who he was going to marry. But suddenly after seeing Banks move on, he wasn't happy anymore.

He called the romance off.

His lady was devastated.

He didn't give a fuck.

To pass time, he and Joey created a tequila brand which already got some traction overseas. It was called LouWales. To hear them tell it, it was all about the money, but everyone knew what it was truly about.

Joey was confused.

And Mason was still in love with someone he could never have.

After the wedding Mason sat next to the fire dressed in all white in the lounge. He was drinking whiskey when Banks walked into the room wearing a khaki-colored linen short set.

Mason was shocked to see him.

"Shouldn't you be with your new wife? It's your wedding day."

"Why would I be with her?" He looked at his watch. "Don't we normally be on our third glass by now? If you ask me, I'm late."

Mason got up and poured him a glass and then reclaimed his seat. "So how does it feel to be married? Again?" He laughed.

Banks sipped easy. "I don't think I really thought about it until now. But it feels the same."

Mason frowned. "Explain."

Banks sat the glass down on the brass martini table. "I thought having a wife would make all of this complete." He looked around. "You know that settled feeling old people often talk about."

Mason nodded.

"But I think I was already good." He looked at him directly in his eyes. "You know what I mean?"

Mason smiled. "You aren't trying to get an annulment already are you?" He chuckled.

276

"Nope. Faye's a good woman. She's smart and can help me on the business side of things. But I can honestly say no matter what goes on in my life, as long as we're good, I'm good too."

"You just finding that shit out?"

They sipped in peace.

"So...you ever think about Ace?" Mason shook the glass, rattling his ice cubes awake. "And what we did to him?"

"Sometimes. But each day it's less." He paused. "The alternative was to kill him."

Mason nodded. "True."

"What about you?" Banks took a larger sip.

"I gotta be honest...every day."

Bank sat back, neither knowing that as they spoke, Ace was landing in America.

CABELLO SALVAJE

The small row home in Prince George's County Maryland was well kept on the outside, to conceal its freakish acts on the inside.

Run by a small black woman who was born into sexual servitude, before killing her captors and starting her own whorehouse, it was known as a well-established and respectful brothel.

The women who worked there all had larger plans for life.

Excuses for some.

A reason to do what they felt necessary, for many.

Some were selling their bodies to go to college. Some were taking care of their children. And others had given up on life and their souls, and as a result, didn't care what happened to them.

The latter story was that of Arbella Valentine.

After realizing her father had brainwashed her for greed, which Banks awarded him $500,000, she decided she would cut him off for good. The thing was, he had taken every cent she owned from the insurance money and offered no intention of giving it back.

Putting her in a financial bind.

This was only compounded by not being able to find Ace Wales. She searched high and low for him and even tried to locate his family before learning from someone deep in the streets that the billionaires had gone back to Belize.

By T. Styles

Arbella cried for six months straight upon hearing the news.

Her heart was broken because Ace never returned for her.

Maybe he died after all. She thought, crying many nights.

But Arbella was strong, and so she worked two to three jobs to make ends meet, with the sole focus on opening another store. She was done with love and everything it represented. The plan was to be all about her work.

And then her mother died.

This was the push that changed her life forever.

First, she missed two days of work, followed by three and four each week due to drinking so much. Before long she lost all her jobs and was so irresponsible, she couldn't hold another longer than a week.

It was at that time that she met Ocean, a girl with a smooth-talking voice, and lies wrapped in visions for the future.

For the past year that Arbella had been working for her, she slept with so many men that at one point she couldn't tell one face from another.

This was her current situation.

He wasn't a client...he was something to do.

After satisfying a man, who preferred to be smacked while being ridden in her room, she lay in bed, thinking about her life. She couldn't wait for her shift to be over so she could drink her troubles away.

Standing in front of the mirror, she brushed her long hair.

Her beauty remained untapped, although she knew that was just a matter of time. After all, she was an alcoholic.

When the door unlocked, Ocean walked inside. For her to be so powerful, her height always shocked people who first met her, because she was so small. "You have another client."

She nodded. "Give me five minutes."

Ocean winked and walked out.

First Arbella made the bed. This was an act the other girls thought was dumb. "Them niggas don't care about them dry ass sheets," they would say. "All they care about is a glossy ass pussy."

But Arbella did care.

And so she had her processes.

There were two things that she would always do. First, change the sheets after each session and next wash up to get the last man off her body.

After showering and drying off in the bathroom, she heard the door open in her room. She knew her client was waiting. "I'll be just a minute!"

"*No problem*," he said in Spanish.

With her hands planted on the sink she looked at herself in the foggy mirror. "One more and done."

Taking a deep breath, when she opened the door leading from her bathroom, she dropped to her knees at what she was seeing. Ace was standing by the door, hair low with a connecting beard that made him look prestigious.

He smelled fresh.

Looked great.

And she felt unworthy.

Still, notwithstanding time, he stared at her as he had many years ago despite his eyes being filled with darkness.

Oddly enough, he looked like, young Banks. Filled with vision, mystery, and dangerous focus.

Slowly he walked up to her, lifted her up and cradled her in his arms. If he hadn't, Arbella would not have been able to move from the floor.

Sitting on the foot of the bed, he looked down at the true love of his life. To the point, Ace had never slept with another woman since he had last been with her.

"I don't want you to see me like this," she said, hiding her face.

"Baby..." his voice was heavy. "Look at me."

"I can't."

"No, Ace, please stop."

"Cabello."

She looked at him now. "Cabello?"

"Listen to me," he said seriously. "I have thought about you every day since the last time I saw your face. Your love was the only thing that got me through."

"But I've been using...my body...for money."

"I won't charge you for what you did before me. It's about what you do after." He kissed her lips. "But I must be honest, I have a son."

Her heart rocked. "Ace...I mean...how?"

"Before I left I made a move I'm ashamed of. And I'm going to get my son and make it right. His name is Roman. Can you deal with that?"

"I don't want any woman in the picture if I do, Cabello. If he be yours, you must let me raise him as my own."

By T. Styles

"Done. I would kill her and dump her before I let her come between us. And that goes for anybody else too."

The embrace, the threats of violence and his undying love restored her heart to its rightful place.

"I must be honest again, what happened to me won't be right until I make a few moves," he said seriously. "Against the family."

She noticed his voice was heavily accented, and she loved every bit of it.

"Okay."

"Are you willing to ride no matter what?"

"Never again will I allow anyone to come between us. That includes my father, or anybody else in the streets. I saw what it was like living without you. And it brought me to my knees."

He smiled and kissed her lips again.

Slowly she stood before him and then straddled him. Placing cool hands on the sides of his face she said, "Now what do you want to do?"

"First, I wanna rob this place. Then outside of fucking you, it's time to take over the world."

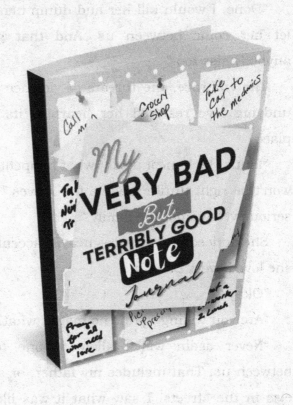

Visit:
www.theelitewritersacademy.com

For Planners, Courses and Templates

By T. Styles

CARTEL PUBLICATIONS

PRESENTS

The Cartel Publications Order Form

www.thecartelpublications.com

Inmates **ONLY** receive novels for $12.00 per book **PLUS** shipping fee **PER BOOK.**

(Mail Order **MUST** come from inmate directly to receive discount)

Shyt List 1		$15.00
Shyt List 2		$15.00
Shyt List 3		$15.00
Shyt List 4		$15.00
Shyt List 5		$15.00
Shyt List 6		$15.00
Pitbulls In A Skirt		$15.00
Pitbulls In A Skirt 2		$15.00
Pitbulls In A Skirt 3		$15.00
Pitbulls In A Skirt 4		$15.00
Pitbulls In A Skirt 5		$15.00
Victoria's Secret		$15.00
Poison 1		$15.00
Poison 2		$15.00
Hell Razor Honeys		$15.00
Hell Razor Honeys 2		$15.00
A Hustler's Son		$15.00
A Hustler's Son 2		$15.00
Black and Ugly		$15.00
Black and Ugly As Ever		$15.00
Ms Wayne & The Queens of DC **(LGBTQ)**		$15.00
Black And The Ugliest		$15.00
Year Of The Crackmom		$15.00
Deadheads		$15.00
The Face That Launched A Thousand Bullets		$15.00
The Unusual Suspects		$15.00
Paid In Blood		$15.00
Raunchy		$15.00
Raunchy 2		$15.00
Raunchy 3		$15.00
Mad Maxxx (4th Book Raunchy Series)		$15.00
Quita's Dayscare Center		$15.00
Quita's Dayscare Center 2		$15.00
Pretty Kings		$15.00
Pretty Kings 2		$15.00
Pretty Kings 3		$15.00
Pretty Kings 4		$15.00
Silence Of The Nine		$15.00
Silence Of The Nine 2		$15.00

Silence Of The Nine 3	_____	$15.00
Prison Throne	_____	$15.00
Drunk & Hot Girls	_____	$15.00
Hersband Material **(LGBTQ)** _ _____		$15.00
The End: How To Write A _____		$15.00
Bestselling Novel In 30 Days (Non-Fiction Guide)		
Upscale Kittens	_____	$15.00
Wake & Bake Boys	_____	$15.00
Young & Dumb	_____	$15.00
Young & Dumb 2: Vyce's Getback	_____	$15.00
Tranny 911 **(LGBTQ)**	_____	$15.00
Tranny 911: Dixie's Rise **(LGBTQ)** _____		
$15.00		
First Comes Love, Then Comes Murder _____		$15.00
Luxury Tax	_____	$15.00
The Lying King	_____	$15.00
Crazy Kind Of Love	_____	$15.00
Goon	_____	$15.00
And They Call Me God	_____	$15.00
The Ungrateful Bastards	_____	$15.00
Lipstick Dom **(LGBTQ)**	_____	$15.00
A School of Dolls **(LGBTQ)**	_____	$15.00
Hoetic Justice	_____	$15.00
KALI: Raunchy Relived	_____	$15.00
(5th Book in Raunchy Series)		
Skeezers	_____	$15.00
Skeezers 2	_____	$15.00
You Kissed Me, Now I Own You	_____	$15.00
Nefarious	_____	$15.00
Redbone 3: The Rise of The Fold	_____	$15.00
The Fold (4th Redbone Book)	_____	$15.00
Clown Niggas	_____	$15.00
The One You Shouldn't Trust	_____	$15.00
The WHORE The Wind		
Blew My Way	_____	$15.00
She Brings The Worst Kind	_____	$15.00
The House That Crack Built	_____	$15.00
The House That Crack Built 2	_____	15.00
The House That Crack Built 3	_____	$15.00
The House That Crack Built 4	_____	$15.00
Level Up **(LGBTQ)**	_____	$15.00
Villains: It's Savage Season	_____	$15.00
Gay For My Bae	_____	$15.00
War	_____	$15.00
War 2: All Hell Breaks Loose	_____	$15.00
War 3: The Land Of The Lou's	_____	$15.00
War 4: Skull Island	_____	$15.00
War 5: Karma	_____	$15.00
War 6: Envy	_____	$15.00
War 7: Pink Cotton	_____	$15.00
Madjesty vs. Jayden (Novella) _____		$8.99
You Left Me No Choice	_____	$15.00
Truce – A War Saga (War 8)	_____	$15.00
Ask The Streets For Mercy	_____	$15.00
Truce 2 (War 9)	_____	$15.00
An Ace and Walid Very, Very Bad Christmas (War 10) _____		$15.00
Truce 3 – The Sins of The Fathers (War 11) _____		$15.00
Truce 4: The Finale (War 12)	_____	$15.00
Treason	_____	$20.00
Treason 2	_____	$20.00
Hersband Material 2 **(LGBTQ)** _____		$15.00
The Gods Of Everything Else (War 13) _____		$15.00

The Gods Of Everything Else 2 (War 14) _____ $15.00

(**Redbone 1 & 2** are **NOT** Cartel Publications novels and if <u>**ordered**</u> the cost is **FULL** price of $16.00 **each plus shipping. <u>No Exceptions</u>.**)

Please add **$7.00** for shipping and handling fees for up to **(2) BOOKS PER ORDER**. (INMATES INCLUDED) (See next page for details)

The Cartel Publications * P.O. BOX 486 OWINGS MILLS MD 21117

Name: _____

Address: _____

City/State: _____

Contact/Email: _____

Please allow 10-15 BUSINESS days Before shipping.

***PLEASE NOTE DUE TO <u>COVID-19</u> SOME ORDERS MAY TAKE UP TO <u>3 WEEKS</u> <u>OR LONGER</u>
BEFORE THEY SHIP***

The Cartel Publications is <u>NOT</u> responsible for <u>Prison Orders</u> rejected!

<u>NO RETURNS and NO REFUNDS</u>
<u>NO PERSONAL CHECKS ACCEPTED</u>
<u>STAMPS NO LONGER ACCEPTED</u>